Dark Starry Morning

Stories of this world and beyond

David Patneaude

Albert Whitman & Company
Morton Grove, Illinois

To my mom and dad, who chased away the Slurpers of my childhood and lit my path through the shadow canyon.

Also by David Patneaude
Someone Was Watching

Library of Congress Cataloging-in-Publication Data
Patneaude, David.
Dark starry morning : stories of this world and beyond / written by David Patneaude.
p.   cm.
ISBN 0-8075-1474-8
I. Title.
PS3566.A7795D37 1995
813'.54—dc20

95-770
CIP

10   9   8   7   6   5   4   3   2   1

The text of this book is set in Goudy
Design by Sandy Newell

Dark Starry Morning

I should've known something strange was going on when I first noticed the headlights. The bus was moving back and forth across the highway, straddling the center line. But I just figured old Mooney had had another long night over a tall bottle. My mind was on other things, anyway: parents who stopped fighting only when they were ganging up on me; a Christmas that had been heavy on bills and light on presents; going back to school after a winter vacation that seemed too short; a seventh-grade English project that was due, but not done. And to top it all off, my mom had just told me for the last and final and absolutely final time, that I wouldn't be going to Central for basketball camp that summer. That it had been a tough year for the Christmas tree business. That my dad's real job—his logging job—might be gone for good. That unless I could raise the three hundred dollars myself, I was out of luck.

But where was a thirteen-year-old kid supposed to

raise three hundred bucks in six months on the Olympic Peninsula? A paper route, when the houses were a mile apart? Babysitting, when there was nowhere to go and no money to spend? I told her there was no way, and I told her some other things, too, until my dad told me to shut my mouth. That was when I left. That was why I left early. That was why I was wishing I could leave for good. And why I'd been standing out in the cold long enough to soak up a couple pounds of rainwater, to watch as the clouds cleared and left the sky black and layered with stars.

So I didn't really notice the bus that much. But as it snaked closer, I stepped onto the shoulder into a clump of tall grass. I felt the blades shed their coat of water on the legs of my pants. The cold wetness seeped through my socks. I cursed out loud and waited for the bus to come.

It stopped with a hiss and a squeal, half on the road, half off, leaning crazily. At first the doors didn't open, and through the foggy, rain-splattered glass, I could see the driver struggling with the controls. Old Mooney had had a tough night.

Finally, the doors creaked open, and when I stepped on, I noticed the guy behind the wheel didn't look at all like old Mooney, who was a short, bald, white guy with a red face. This driver was tall, with long, straight, black hair, and dark skin—Michael Jordan dark. He had one of those Egyptian noses—long and narrow—and he reminded me of an old pharoah. Except he had this big smile on his face, and I don't remember ever seeing a picture of a smiling pharoah.

"Welcome, Thomas," he said in a deep voice—thunder deep—and he held up his hand in a kind of stiff salute.

How did this guy know my name? Maybe they had some kind of master list somewhere. "Where's Mr. Mooney?" I said as the doors closed behind me.

"Mr. Mooney?" he said. The words sounded different. Some kind of accent, but I couldn't place it. "Mr. Mooney sick. Mr. Mooney have bad night." And then he laughed—a loud, echoing drumroll of a laugh that made me want to join in. It came from way down in his chest and turned his whole face into a smile.

I kept an eagle eye on him and turned for the back of the bus, where I usually sat with the Roper twins, a couple of guys who lived on a tree farm a mile or so down the highway. They were first to be picked up, I was second. But the rear of the bus was empty. I decided to stay put. If this guy was going to drive off the road or something, I'd need to get out in a hurry. I picked the third seat behind him and slid over by the window.

"Where are the Ropers?" I said.

"The Ropers? They sick. Flu." He laughed that laugh again.

"Both of them?"

He grinned at me. "Twins—they do everything together."

The bus jerked away from the shoulder, heading for the center line as it accelerated through the dark.

I sat there for a moment not saying anything, getting nervous. "Why are you driving down the middle of the road?"

"Stay out of ditch."

"What if a car comes the other way?"

He looked up at me in the big rearview mirror, and I could see his smile. He took his hands off the wheel and brought them together in a thunderous clap. The bus veered toward the shoulder on the opposite side of the road. "Boom!" he said in a loud voice, and laughed.

Was this guy kidding? He had to be, didn't he? I leaned forward in my seat, edged toward the aisle, ready to spring up if I needed to, wishing that the bus had seat belts, wishing that I'd never gotten on it.

The driver pressed down on the gas, and the bus picked up speed. Up the road, headlights appeared as a car came toward us from around a corner. I got to my feet, ready to move, to get to the back of the bus, where I wouldn't be crunched like a peanut in a shell.

But the bus moved over. I sat back down.

"How your vacation, Thomas?" I could see his eyes on me in the mirror.

"It sucked." I wondered if they had that expression where he came from.

"Sucked." A pause, then the laugh again.

I guessed that they didn't have it.

"You like school, Thomas?"

"It sucks."

"Sucks." He turned to look at me, cackling, and the bus veered toward the shoulder again. "You funny guy, Thomas."

"Keep your eyes on the road." I rose up out of my seat again, ready to make a run for it.

He grinned and turned back to the windshield, and the bus angled back to the center line.

"You think everything's funny?" I said.

Another grin. "Not everything."

The bus continued on down the highway. Another car came, and we moved over, and I breathed a little easier. "You from around here?" I don't know why I asked. I knew he wasn't.

"Just came."

"From where?"

"Many places." He took both hands off the wheel, held his arms wide until the bus started to drift.

I waited for him to say more, but he didn't. I sat back in the seat and looked out the windshield at our headlights cutting through the dark.

The bus slowed. "Next passenger," he said, grinning at me in the mirror.

I looked ahead to the right shoulder and saw a tiny red light flame up and then dim again. Eleanor Ransom was having her morning cigarette. The bus creaked to a stop, right wheels on the shoulder, and the doors opened. But she didn't get on. From where I was sitting I couldn't see her, but I could picture her out there, sucking in hard on those last couple of drags.

"Welcome, Eleanor," the driver said. He smiled out into the darkness.

"Who are you?" I heard her say over the noise of the motor.

"The new bus guy." He laughed, loud and long.

"You got a name, Laughing Man?" I saw her cigarette butt arc into the air like a flare, and she stepped onto the bus. She stood next to him, rain shining on her black hair. She looked at his face, studying him, or trying to stare him down, maybe, waiting for an answer.

"Vasco," he said. "Name is Vasco."

"Vasco? That's worse than Eleanor."

"Eleanor is pretty name."

"So's Vasco."

"So's Vasco." He chuckled, low and rumbly. "So's Vasco. You funny, Eleanor."

Eleanor gave him that Eleanor look, rough as fir bark, hard as river rock. But when she turned and walked toward me, I could see a little light in her dark eyes, a little grin at the corners of her mouth.

"Eleanor," I said. I shrugged my shoulders to let her know that I didn't know what to make of him either.

"Hi, Tommy," she said. She was wearing even more makeup than usual, but I could see a big bruise that ran from under her right eye down her cheek. Her old man must've been slapping her around again. She sat in the seat across the aisle from me and turned toward the window.

"Have a good vacation?" I said.

"Same old story," she said. "When my dad ain't working, he drinks. When he drinks, he hits me. He ain't working. He ain't worked in months."

She turned and looked at me with those Eleanor eyes. She didn't have a fourteen-year-old face. She was a year older than I was, but she looked more like five years older. I could see tears forming, but she wiped them away with a swipe of her sleeve.

"You have good vacation, Eleanor?" Vasco said. His voice carried back to us like he was on a loudspeaker. He turned and smiled at her, and the bus crossed the center line and swerved toward the ditch on the other side before he got it back to the middle of the road.

"Nice driving," Eleanor said.

"Thank you," he said. "And your vacation?"

"Great," Eleanor said.

"Great," he said, and laughed.

"Why'd you tell him my name?" she said to me.

"I didn't. They must have some kind of list or something."

"Sure. And Laughing Man memorized it."

"He must've. Wait till he stops for Stevenson, and you'll see. I bet he knows his name, too."

"We'll see," Eleanor said.

I watched Vasco look in his rearview mirror. "You folks been traveling much?" he said.

"Back and forth to school," I said. "That's about it."

"Back and forth to foster homes," Eleanor said. "That's about it."

Vasco's shoulders shook with laughter. "You guys like travel?"

"You gonna take us to Hawaii?" Eleanor said.

"On the bus?" I said.

Vasco laughed.

I looked through the windshield. We were getting close to Mike Stevenson's stop. Vasco should've been backing off, moving to the right. Instead, the bus kept rolling along, straddling the yellow stripe.

"You got a stop coming up here," Eleanor said.

"Yeah," I said. "You better slow this thing down."

Vasco turned and grinned at us.

Mike was up ahead, standing on the shoulder, lit up by the headlights. We got closer, and I could see him staring at the bus. As we raced past him, full speed, kicking up water from the road, his mouth fell open, his head swiveled to follow us. He raised his hand. But all he got was a faceful of wind and water, and as I looked back at him, his baseball hat flew off and landed in the ditch.

A rumble of laughter rose from the front.

"What are you doing?" Eleanor said.

"You were supposed to pick him up," I said.

"He walk."

"It's ten miles!" I said.

"Walk fast."

"His old man's the school superintendent," Eleanor said. "You're gonna be in trouble."

"Don't think so," Vasco said. He turned and smiled at us, and I suddenly knew the Roper twins weren't really sick. I could see them standing in the cold, wondering why the bus had passed them by. And what about old Mooney? Was he back at the school, looking for his bus?

I didn't like this. I looked over at Eleanor, but her eyes were straight ahead, on Vasco. "You ain't a real bus driver," she said. "Just let us out here. We'll walk the rest of the way." That Eleanor edge, sharpened on the streets, was in her voice. She was trying to be tough, but I could feel the fear in her, too.

"Too far," Vasco said. "Much too far." He grinned into the mirror.

"We'll walk fast," Eleanor said.

"Walk fast. You funny, Eleanor." The laugh rolled out, bounced off the bare insides of the bus.

I glanced at Eleanor, expecting her to make a move. She wouldn't put up with much more of this. And I was ready to follow her—almost. But something about Vasco—his laugh, maybe, his eyes—made me as much curious as scared. Somehow I felt that he wasn't going to hurt us—on purpose, anyway. And Eleanor must've felt the same thing. She'd leaned back on her seat and was rummaging through her backpack.

The bus raced along another mile or so. Vasco jammed on the brake and took a hard right onto a Forest Service road. The right rear wheel caught the edge of the ditch, and the bus bounced and lurched before heading up the narrow road.

"Where are you going?" I said. Suddenly I wanted out.

"Detour," Vasco said. "Scenic route."

I turned to Eleanor. She was putting a cigarette in her mouth, lighting it. She held up the pack to me, but I shook my head. I could barely breathe as it was.

Vasco looked in the mirror. "Bad for you," he said. Eleanor inhaled deeply and blew a stream of smoke in his direction. "Bad for you, Eleanor." He got his eyes back on the road as we started up an incline. Eleanor kept smoking.

The road zig-zagged back and forth, narrowing until the mirrors on the bus were grazing branches and brush on both sides. I struggled out of my seat, holding on to the seatback in front of me, looking to see if Vasco had some kind of weapon. Maybe I'd been wrong. Maybe he was going to do something to us.

I sat back down, gripping the old vinyl seat as hard as I could. I hadn't seen any weapon, but so what?

Eleanor ground her cigarette butt into the floor and reached across the aisle, put her hand over mine. I must've looked more scared than I felt. Maybe she was more afraid than she looked. Her hand felt good—cool and soft.

"This guy's okay," she said, staring into his eyes in the mirror. How did she know that?

"How much farther?" I asked Vasco. I sounded like some kid on a car trip with his parents. But I wasn't sure I wanted to get there—wherever "there" was. I was trying to think of some way to get off the bus while it was moving. Halfway back in the bus was an emergency exit, but I'd never used it. I didn't know how to use it. I didn't know if I could. And what would I miss if I did somehow escape?

I didn't have to think about it for long. We came to the top of the hill and hit a level spot. It was lighter outside, and I could see the trees had thinned out. To our left, beyond a shallow row of tall firs, was a clearing. The bus slowed until it was creeping along the road like a slug. Then it stopped. I figured we were in trouble.

Vasco glanced at his watch. "Perfect," he said.

I looked at Eleanor. She smiled, but she didn't look happy. She got up and sat next to me, squeezed my hand until it hurt. But I didn't want to let go. I looked at her, and then away. I didn't know what to say. But something made me look at her again. Something strange was happening to her. Her hair, still wet from the rain, was starting to stick up, to stand out in little spikey strands all over her head. She looked like the coyote in a Roadrunner cartoon after he'd taken about ten thousand volts from one of his inventions. She must have felt it, or seen me staring at it, or both, because she reached up with both hands and grabbed onto the spikes of hair, trying to push them back down. I watched an amazed smile cross her face, and then she laughed, and I knew she was looking at *my* hair. I reached up and touched it. It was standing on end, and my scalp tingled. My whole body tingled.

Vasco turned around. His hair had formed a black semi-circle around his head. He laughed. "You guys sure look funny."

Eleanor stopped smiling. "What did you do to the bus?" she said. "Did you screw up the electrical system?"

Vasco grinned. "Electrical system?"

Something beyond the trees—in the clearing—caught my eye. I turned to the foggy window and wiped it off with my sleeve. What was that thing? I got closer and closer to the window, until my cheek and nose were pressed against the glass. I could feel Eleanor hovering over my right shoulder, her bushy hair brushing my face, her perfume—sweet and strong—alive in my nostrils, in my brain.

"What is it?" she said.

"I don't know." It looked like a big ball, more than half the height of the tallest nearby tree. It was dark at first, but then glowing—a glow that seemed to come from within, right through its skin, or shell, or whatever it was that made up the outside.

The glow got brighter—a shade of green I didn't

remember ever seeing before—and I felt the hair on my arms bristle.

Vasco opened the door and turned off the engine. Its rumble was replaced by a faint hum coming from the direction of the globe. He stood and held his hand out toward the open door. "Time to go," he said with a smile. "She ready for us."

"We ain't going anywhere," Eleanor said. Her hand pressed down on my knee, pinning me to the seat.

"What is that thing?" I said. It had to be a hundred feet away, but its soft green light filled the inside of the bus.

"Come," Vasco said. His smile was still there. It looked permanent.

"You go ahead," Eleanor said. "I'll just drive Tommy and me back in the bus."

"You drive bus?" He laughed. "Too young, Eleanor."

"I can drive better than you."

"She waiting," Vasco said. Eleanor and I just sat there. I looked at her, searching for some kind of clue that she had a plan—that she had an idea of what we should do.

Vasco turned toward the ball and stared at it a moment. "She comes."

"Who comes?" Eleanor said.

Vasco gestured toward the clearing. "There."

I looked where he was pointing. I could see someone walking toward the bus, silhouetted against the
glowing green background. It looked like a woman, tall
and slender, walking fast. Behind her, a rectangular
opening had appeared at the base of the ball. I couldn't
believe what I was seeing.

"Space people," Eleanor said. I thought she'd be
afraid; I was afraid. But there was only wonder in her
voice. "These guys are from space."

Vasco smiled back at her.

"Are you?" I asked Vasco. Maybe they were just
making a movie up here. Maybe they wanted us to be
in it.

"No movies," Vasco said. And I knew he was right;
actors didn't read minds.

"Why'd you bring us here?" Eleanor said. Her voice
had lost its tough crust. She was barely whispering.

"Come," Vasco said. "Meet her." With both hands,
he gently motioned us to the front of the bus, and I
followed Eleanor as she got out of the seat and walked
toward him.

Suddenly the woman stepped to the top of the bus's
stairwell and stood facing us, smiling. She laughed, but
it wasn't a Vasco laugh. It was soft and musical, like
wind chimes on a spring morning. "Did you frighten
them, Vasco?"

"Quite likely, Amelia. My ways need improvement."

"You did fine. Why don't you see to the craft."

"Yes." Vasco headed down the steps and out the door, and for a moment I watched him walk toward the globe, his long strides eating up ground.

"Why are we here?" Eleanor said. The woman—Amelia—had a friendly smile, a reassuring smile. She looked much like Vasco—dark hair, dark skin, tall and angular. From three feet away I could see the color of her eyes, the same shade of green that filled the clearing and lit the bus.

"You are here because you are not happy with your lives on this world. We would like to take you to a better place."

Eleanor was looking at this woman as if she was trying to see past those green eyes. "You mean to another planet?"

"Yes. A planet with no sickness or poverty, no hunger or fear or prejudice, no hatred or war." She looked intently at Eleanor's face. "Or abuse."

Vasco appeared at the door. "Or death," he said. He spread his arms wide and smiled. "Live forever."

"You mean nobody dies?" I said.

"Sometimes in bad accident," Vasco said. "Then we can't fix."

"You mean, like if you're riding with a real bad bus

driver?" Eleanor said.

"Bad bus driver," Vasco repeated, and laughed.

I thought about living forever—never dying. Did they really have a way to make it so I'd never die? Was their world really as good as they said?

"Can we come back here if we don't like it?" Eleanor said. "Can we ever come back?"

"You can, but we don't come this way very often," Amelia said. "And no one has ever wanted to return."

"Other kids have gone with you?" I said.

"Missing persons, you call them," Amelia said. "Children and adults. There are others coming with us now, waiting for you in the craft. You are the last."

"How many?" Eleanor said.

"Thirteen, counting you and Thomas," Amelia said. "All children this time."

Thirteen, I thought. An unlucky number. And I'd never even had enough nerve to hitchhike; how could I think about going away—forever—with these two strangers? But how could I pass up the chance to go— to live on a planet where nothing bad ever happened, where you would never want to die, and you wouldn't have to?

"How'd we get so lucky?" Eleanor said. "Thirteen from a whole planet, and you picked us? What about the starving kids, the dying kids?"

"This our sector of Earth, Eleanor," Vasco said. "More of us in other places."

"There are many kinds of starvation," Amelia said. "Many kinds of dying. The famished and sick are as plentiful as the trees on these hills. If our planet had more room, we would take more. But to us a wounded heart is as unfortunate as a shrunken stomach or a withered limb. And we found you."

I remembered what had happened earlier that morning—how I had wished I could get out of my house forever. This was my chance. But then I thought about my parents, who'd taken one beating after another lately. Lose me now? I was all they had. How could I leave them? How could I be happy someplace far away without them? And I really wasn't that unhappy here. Things would get better.

"How did you know we were unhappy?" I said to Amelia.

She tapped her forehead. "You talked; we heard you."

"I didn't mean it," I said. Suddenly I felt panicky. Would they make me go with them?

Amelia stared into my eyes until I had to look away. Then she smiled. "You didn't mean it, did you, Thomas?"

I shook my head.

"And you, Eleanor? What is your decision?"

"Is there anything I won't like about it up there?" she said. I wanted to tell her not to even think about it, but I couldn't come up with a reason. She had nothing here.

"I think you will like everything." Amelia said. "You will have family and friends."

"One thing," Vasco said. "No smoking. Eleanor cannot smoke."

Eleanor pulled the pack of cigarettes from her coat pocket. She crumpled it up in one hand and dropped it on the floor. She smiled at Vasco, and I saw a light in her eyes that I'd never seen before.

"You come, Eleanor?" Vasco said. "You come with us?"

"Will I have to laugh?" Eleanor said.

"Will I have to laugh." Vasco chuckled.

"You will want to, Eleanor," Amelia said.

"I'm coming," Eleanor said.

Vasco laughed his laugh, but it was louder this time, and longer, rolling on like the explosions from a string of dynamite sticks.

Amelia gave Eleanor a big hug, and Eleanor hugged her back. I stood there feeling left out. Was it too late to change my mind? Amelia looked at me. She could hear what I was thinking.

But I shook my head. I couldn't go. I couldn't.

"As for Thomas," Amelia said, "he needs to get back."

"We can take him," Vasco said.

On the craft? I looked at Vasco. "You know where my house is?"

"Near bus stop," Vasco said. "Sundquist on mailbox. Long gravel driveway to house. Many small trees."

"If you keep going down the driveway, past the house, past the small trees, there's a stand of big trees. Thick. Nobody could see in. A quarter mile into the big trees, there's an old shed in a clearing. You could land the craft there."

I had the feeling Vasco was looking into my mind. "I know the place," he said. "No problem."

Up close the globe looked bigger. Its glow turned our faces into halloween masks as we approached. Eleanor walked next to me, but her steps were impatient. I could tell she wanted to run ahead.

We walked up a ramp into a small, bare, dimly lit room. The ceiling was low, and another door—closed tight—was centered on the wall straight ahead.

Amelia pushed a button on the wall, and the ramp came up, forming a door, sealing out the outside. "We are going inside, but you will remain in this chamber. When the door goes back down, you may get out."

Eleanor looked at me, a smile in her eyes, and then a question. "You sure, Tommy?" She put her hand on my arm. Her face was alive with happiness, and I knew she'd made the right decision.

But what about me? What about my decision? "I can't go, Eleanor," I said.

She gave me a quick hug—a touch of her cheek, a whiff of her perfume—and turned to Amelia and Vasco. "I'm ready," she said.

Vasco looked at me. "You have a good life, Thomas," he said.

"Will you be back?" I said.

"Quite likely," Vasco said.

"Can you find me again?"

"You found us," Amelia said. "If your thoughts are strong enough, you can find us again, and we will come to you."

"We can find your home again," Vasco said. "You stay there, we find you."

I thought about spending the rest of my life on the tree farm, waiting for Vasco and Amelia to come back. Not a great prospect, but if nothing better came along, I could live with it. And maybe someday when my parents were gone or didn't need me any longer, I'd get another chance. Maybe I'd take it next time. "Look for me," I said. "Just don't come in a bus."

Vasco laughed and hugged me, and I could feel the strength in his arms. Then he turned and pushed some buttons on the wall, and the door to the interior opened. It was nearly dark on the inside, lit only by a cloudy green glow. I couldn't make out anything.

"Good-bye, Thomas," Amelia said. She turned toward Vasco and Eleanor. Together they walked through the door. Eleanor didn't look back. I watched the door slide shut and stood there waiting.

The light in the room dimmed until it was nearly dark. The outside door opened, and I wondered what was going on. We hadn't gone anywhere yet.

But I looked out, and we were there. I could see the trees, a corner of the shed. I walked down the ramp to the wet grass. The door was already closed by the time I turned around. But the craft didn't take off—not that I could see, anyway. One second it was there, big and round and glowing its green glow. The next it was gone—no movement, no sound—and for a moment I thought maybe I'd imagined the whole thing. But I knew I hadn't.

I walked down the driveway. I needed to get to the road and wait for that school bus, and then go back home and tell my mom and dad that old Mooney must have had a long night, that I needed a ride to school.

• • •

When I made my decision, I hoped that I'd be
happy with it, and I have been—most of the time. But
more often than I like, I think about what might have
been: when I notice new lines around my mom's eyes or
a stoop in my dad's shoulders, and picture myself getting wrinkled and bent under the weight of too much
worry and too little hope; when the school bus arrives
in the morning, and the driver is a little slow getting
the doors opened; when we pass Eleanor's stop, and the
bus doesn't even slow down. I imagine the red glow
from her cigarette as it flares and then arcs into the sky.
I look up, following it, and on a clear, dark, starry
morning, I can sometimes see a green light moving
through the heavens. I know I can.

A Melody For Mizorca

Cort's dad stared at his morning paper and whistled, low and drawn out. Cort put his cereal spoon down and waited. His mom was waiting, too. Even Cort's baby brother, Dougie, stopped drinking his juice and looked at his dad.

Cort watched tears form in the corners of his dad's eyes and trickle down the sides of his nose. He hadn't seen him cry in a long time—not since Grandpa died.

"They've found an orca," his dad said. "Alive." His voice was hoarse and shaky.

A norca. Cort wasn't sure what that was, but it sounded familiar. Something from school, maybe.

Then he remembered, or thought he did. "Isn't a norca some kind of dinosaur or somethin', Dad?" he said. "That lived in the ocean?"

"Orca, Cort," his dad said. "O-R-C-A. The largest member of the dolphin family. Killer whales, they called them. But they weren't, really. Except for their food, of course."

Cort tried to imagine what kind of food killer whales would eat. Whatever they wanted, probably.

His mom glanced at the paper. Her eyebrows peaked like little boomerangs.

"How long ago did they live?" Cort said.

"Fifty years ago they were still being seen in Puget Sound," his dad said. "Your grandpa saw some once when he was out fishing with his dad." He stood up. "Wait here a minute," he said.

Fishing? Cort thought. You could fish in Puget Sound?

Cort's mom passed him the paper. The headlines and article took up half the front page of *The Times*. But the picture was what got his attention. Right under the headline, WHALE CAPTURED, and in smaller print, THOUGHT EXTINCT FOR FORTY YEARS, was a picture of an old fishing boat towing a floating pen through the water. And inside a dark, curved fin, shiny wet, pointed skyward.

"Take a look at this, Cort." His dad was back, setting a faded blue book in front of him. *Whales*, it said on the cover. "Page thirty-two," his dad said.

Cort found page thirty-two. A picture. A picture of a banana-shaped black-and-white creature rocketing up out of a calm blue sea. Water cascaded off its smooth skin.

"An orca?" Cort asked.

"An orca," his dad said.

Now it was Cort's turn to whistle. "They lived in the Sound?" he said. "Fifty years ago?" He couldn't believe anything like that had lived in the Sound.

"Before the accident," his dad said. "Before the incident."

"Before the spills," his mom said. "Before the warming."

The accident. The incident. The spills. The warming. Cort had lived his whole twelve years with the aftermath of those events. It was painful for him to think of what had been lost, what he'd never see.

"Where'd they find it, Dad?" he said.

"Off the New Columbia coast. Our government says it was captured in international waters, but the Canadian government thinks it's theirs—they're trying to keep the Americans from bringing it here." He paused and shook his head. "Bringing *her* here, I mean. They say it's a female."

Cort thought about that. He wondered if there was a male out there somewhere. Maybe there could be babies.

He read the killer whale chapter in the book. He read the newspaper article. And he imagined her making the long journey, confined to a cage, alone and confused and afraid. Suddenly he wished he could see her.

All day long the story filled the vid. Reporters and their big-lensed cameras were following her in helicopters and boats. Ms. Orca, they called her now.

And all day long they interviewed government scientists, who tried to explain how she'd survived, where she'd come from, why no one had seen a killer whale in forty years. Some thought that the warming had opened up ice dams that had been sealing off unexplored bays farther north. But all their talk boiled down to one thing: they didn't know for sure.

The scientists were bringing her to Bellingham Bay, where construction was underway on a large pool. Any farther south would be dangerous, they said. And then what? Would they poke and probe and measure and test? And when they'd tired of that, would they lock her up forever in some kind of floating zoo and let people pay to come and gawk at her? Would Cort be one of them? How could he stay away? He felt a lump growing in his throat. He had to get to his room. He had to make some music.

He sat down on his bed, opened the whale book to page thirty-two, and got out his saxophone. For an hour he played, stringing the pieces together one after another. The lump in his throat went away.

The next day she was back in the news. Ms. Orca still. But Dougie called her "Mizorca," like "Missouri." She was on her way down the west coast of Vancouver Island, to a place called Ucluelet, outside Barkley Sound. They were going to make a stop there before continuing on to Washington.

But there were questions about how far she'd get. The Canadian government had filed an official protest, and a war was building between scientists and animal rights groups.

The vid showed her in her cage. She wasn't moving much, but the experts said there wasn't room. They weren't worried.

Cort watched her, fascinated, hoping she'd suddenly submerge, gather her strength, and leap to freedom. But the pen was too shallow. The reporters kept saying she couldn't jump out.

That night he dreamed he was in a boat near her cage, playing his saxophone. First it was mellow music to relax her. And then faster, frenzied. Suddenly she was in the air, high above the wall of her flimsy cage, high above the puny rafts and the puny men with their instruments and cameras.

There was more news the next day, but not good. They were saying that something might be wrong. She hadn't eaten, and she was even less active. And lots of people now were demanding that they set her free. There was even talk about a group planning to do it by force.

"Let's go," Cort's dad said, jumping up from his chair and clicking off the vid.

"What?" Cort's mom said.

"Let's go see her," Cort's dad said. "Before it's too late."

Cort expected his mom to say no.

"Give me a minute to get Dougie's things together, Brad," she said.

"Can I bring my saxophone?" Cort said.

"Hurry and get it," his dad said.

Three hours later they were in Vancouver. From there, they caught a plane to Ucluelet, a run-down village that—according to the pilot—had once thrived on sport fishing and logging, neither of which had survived much past the turn of the century.

Most of the people in town now were visitors—reporters and their crews, writers, scientists, animal and environmental groups, government officials, and people like Cort and his family, who just wanted a chance to see a killer whale.

Cort's dad rented a boat—a forty-two foot cruiser that had seen little use in years. It sat with dozens of others in the harbor, for sale signs posted on their hulls and cabins. But everything on their boat worked, and by early evening they had it loaded with supplies. If Mizorca continued on to Bellingham, Cort's dad planned to follow her.

From where their boat was moored, Cort could look out into the inlet and see boats coming and going. It grew dark, and he followed their lights back and forth. But none was the old fishing boat, towing the pen that held the orca. She was supposed to have been there by now. Cort wondered if she would even come. He went to bed wondering.

It was still dark when his mom woke him up. "She's here," she said. Cort scrambled from his bunk and went out on the deck, where his dad stood, binoculars held to his eyes. Boats circled and reversed their engines and jockeyed for position; bright lights focused on the long refueling dock where the old fishing boat was moored. Behind it, Cort could make out the framework of the pen, and once, as he stared, he thought he saw a flash—a light reflecting off a shiny wet fin. His dad handed him the binoculars. He looked, found the pen, and the fin, moving slowly through the water. "I see her," he said. "I see her."

"They're going to let them go on," his dad said. "At daylight. Then we'll get to see her real well."

"How long till daylight?" Cort said.

His dad looked at his watch. "About two hours."

Two hours. Cort would stay up. He didn't want to miss anything.

A gray dawn had just begun to brighten the harbor when the fishing boat's engine fired up. Cort's dad maneuvered the cruiser away from the dock and out into open water, ready to follow. Five minutes later, the fishing boat towed the pen away and headed out to sea.

"How long will it take?" Cort said.

"To get to Bellingham?" his dad said. "A couple of days, they're saying. That old boat can't go much faster than a crawl with that pen behind it."

A couple of days. Two days and a night with Mizorca. Cort smiled to himself in the gray light.

By the time the procession hit open ocean, Cort's dad had squeezed their boat between two bigger boats carrying reporters and cameras and equipment and had claimed a spot within a rock's throw of the pen. People on the other boats didn't like it—they yelled and cursed and shook their fists as the smaller boat bulled its way in. Cort's dad held up a badge he'd gotten somewhere a long time ago, and shouted something at them about official business. They backed off.

Daylight—gray and filtered by drizzle—arrived, and even without the binoculars Cort could see the orca in her floating cage. Her back—as black and shiny as a wet tire—dipped and rose and slowly weaved from one side of the cage to the other. Her dorsal fin pointed toward the sky like the tail of a rocket. Cort wondered what she was thinking, whether she was scared and lonely. She had to be, he decided. How could they do this to her?

He left his dad and brother on the deck and went to get his saxophone. His mom stood on the flying bridge now, steering the boat, keeping them close. When Cort got back from the cabin, she gave him a wink and smiled. His dad carried Dougie to the rail, where they watched Cort take the sax from its case.

"Play," Dougie said, pointing at the instrument. And Cort did. Soft and slow and mellow at first, and then louder and faster, and louder still.

But she kept moving ahead, drifting from side to side. Slow, rhythmic, unhearing, as if she were in her own world. Maybe the sound meant nothing to her. Maybe the noise from the engines and the water and the shouting voices was drowning out everything else.

Cort put the sax away. But a little while later he got it out again. And then again. By the fourth time his mom had maneuvered the boat a little closer. Cort blew until his lungs hurt, until he was ready to quit.

Suddenly Mizorca stopped her sideways motion. Her head popped up, black and white and glistening, and he could see her mouth, her eyes. She turned toward him, paused so long that he had to stop playing, stop breathing, and just watch her. Slowly she eased back down, resumed her slow drift.

Cort played again, and then once more. But Mizorca didn't react. He wasn't sure that she ever really had.

When it got so dark he couldn't see her anymore, he went to bed. But this time he dreamed of his mom on the flying bridge, suddenly jerking the wheel, steering the boat across the tow ropes at full speed, shredding the lines that held the pen to the fishing boat. She circled back and rammed the cage, collapsing its wall. The cage sank at one end, and Mizorca streaked through the opening, barrel-rolling across the surface as she rocketed past Cort's boat. He looked down at her and caught her big, tooth-filled smile. It was the last thing he saw, the first thing he thought of when he woke up.

Morning brought a hazy sun reflecting on water grown dark and murky. Cort noticed the smell, and the patches of oily film in the troughs between waves. The wake behind the boat was yellow-brown instead of white. He wondered how Mizorca liked this water. He wondered if his mom would really cut through the ropes, if she would really batter down the sides of the pen.

But today his dad was back at the wheel. And the ropes weren't ropes; they were steel cables, thick and shiny. The walls of the cage were sturdy and reinforced. Some dreams didn't come true.

Cort played his saxophone again halfway through the morning, and once more in the early afternoon, but Mizorca didn't respond. She'd even quit moving from side to side. If only everyone would shut off their engines, maybe she'd be able to hear the music. But why would they?

The news guy on the vid said they were getting close to Bellingham. Cort could see the skyline of tall buildings, but he was having a hard time taking his eyes off Mizorca. She'd rolled onto her side at least once, her fin dipping in the water before she righted herself. Something was wrong with her.

A big Coast Guard boat arrived, escorting a smaller boat filled with men and women. Scientists, the vid said. Their boat eased over to the pen, blocking Cort's view.

Then the Coast Guard boat ushered all the other boats—including Cort's—away from the area. By the time they were done being herded, they were trailing the pen by a hundred meters. Cort had to look through the binoculars to see what was going on.

He watched as several people dressed in diving suits

and gear got onto the walls of the cage. Up ahead he could see piers, crowded with people and equipment. A giant crane perched near the end of one pier like a sleeping bird. Mizorca didn't look good. Her dorsal fin swayed and plunged from side to side as if she was fighting to stay upright.

"Let me see the binoculars, Cort." His dad stood next to him with the vid slung over his back. Cort could barely hear the reporter over the noise from the boats. His dad stared through the binoculars at the cage for a long time. "The vid says she's in trouble, Cort," he said finally. "They've got a pool for her—a big one—but I don't know if she's going to make it."

Not going to make it? "Why don't they just let her go?" Cort said. He felt the boat speed up and glanced at his mom on the bridge. She was trying to make up some ground.

"I don't know," his dad said. "I don't think they know how precious that orca is. They still haven't figured it out." He turned up the vid, but the announcer's voice was drowned out by the roar of the engine as Cort's mom closed in on the pen.

The Coast Guard boat was busy up ahead, clearing small craft from the fishing boat's path. Cort couldn't just watch. He had to do something for her. He headed for the cabin to get his saxophone.

When he got back on deck, they were within fifty meters of her. He heard the vid announcer say that the scientists were going to go into the water with her.

On the pier a crowd waited. Trucks and other kinds of equipment competed for space with the people and the crane. Video cameras sat atop tripods, aimed at the approaching boats.

Cort peered through the binoculars. "I don't see her," he said. The pen looked empty. He wouldn't need his saxophone after all. She'd already escaped. Somehow she'd escaped. His heart thumped as he scanned the water for her. Nothing.

His dad took the binoculars back and looked for a long time. And as the fishing boat neared the pier, he made a funny noise in his throat. "She's in the cage," he said, his voice as thin and cold as a new icicle. "On her side."

Men and women jumped into the water, inside the pen. Cort could see Mizorca now, her shiny skin just above the surface. The divers splashed about the cage, scrambling over her like rats. Then they shouted up to the pier, and the crane went into action, lowering a huge sling on the end of its cable. The scientists grabbed the sling and scurried around her, trying to get her into it.

On the vid a newswoman's voice suddenly dropped

from excitement to hushed sincerity. Cort strained to listen.

"Although we've received no official word, an informed source here on the pier tells us that the whale's life signs stopped several minutes ago," she said. "Ms. Orca is dead. The cause is unknown at this time."

"Unknown?" Cort's mom said from the bridge. Her voice was loud but shaky. "How about stupidity?"

Cort's dad stood silently, tears in his eyes, holding Dougie to his chest.

Cort stared at the cage, at the people climbing back over its walls. How could they? he thought. How could they?

The crane whirred and creaked. The cable tightened. Slowly the whale emerged from the water. She was shiny black and white. And still.

A murmur rose from the crowd and died. And was replaced by another sound, soft at first and then stronger, floating across the water to the swaying sling.

Cort's saxophone felt good in his hands—smooth and cool. The music felt right—he'd first heard it at his grandfather's funeral, flowing from the horn of Grandpa's friend Charlie. Cort remembered Charlie's white hair, a red face that glistened with tears, and an Army uniform that was too tight around the middle.

Taps, his mom had called it. Afterward he

remembered the music and practiced it for days, until his dad finally asked him to stop.

But he wasn't asking him to stop now. He nodded to Cort. And his mom smiled a bittersweet, wet-eyed smile. Dougie pointed at the saxophone. "Play," he said. And Cort played it some more. He played it for the animals. For the whales. For Mizorca.

The Wind in My Face

First off, I don't want you to get your hopes up. It's not like some big miracle happened. But *something* did.

Aunt Wendy was my mom's oldest sister, but for the first twelve years of my life, I hardly knew she existed. A card or letter once in a while, a voice on the phone over the holidays, an old family photo (four small kids in the front row and a tall skinny girl in the back with Grandma and Grandpa). That was it.

Then one night my mom and dad turned off the TV and said, "We've got something to tell you," and I knew I was about to get some bad news of one kind or another. I figured we were moving or somebody was losing their job or they were getting a divorce or there was a new kid on the way. Or else they thought it was time to have that Little Talk about boys my mom had been promising me. Yuck! But then what would my dad be doing in the same room? He still thought of me as his little baby girl. So I knew it wasn't the Little Talk.

"Lisa," my mom said, "you know your Uncle Jim and your Aunt Bonnie and Aunt Carrie."

I wasn't sure where she was going with this one. I'd known them all my life. They all lived within five miles of us. "I think I remember them," I said.

She ignored me. "You don't know your Aunt Wendy."

"I've heard of her. Your big sister, right?"

"I haven't seen her in nearly thirty years," my mom said.

"Why?"

"She left, went to do her own thing, pretty much disowned us. How do you like the name Windy?"

"I like it."

"She changed her name to Windy."

"Can you do that?"

My mom's eyebrows pinched closer together. "Not as far as your father and I are concerned."

"So why are you telling me about her now?"

"She has cancer. She's dying."

"And I'll never even get to meet her?"

"You will, Lisa," my dad said.

"She's coming to live with us," my mom said.

Three days later we went to the airport to pick her up. She was ten years older than my mom—almost fifty—and dying, but she looked good. She had that

California tan without a bunch of lines in her face, and a nice figure, and great-looking blond hair. Later on I learned that the hair was a wig—a rug, she called it. The chemo treatments had caused her real hair to fall out.

But her smile was real, and her hugs—big, perfumey ones—were, too. We sat in the back seat on the way home and talked—mostly about me—the whole time. She told me to call her Windy, but the name didn't seem quite right. I called her Auntie. When she said that she thought we were a lot alike, I saw my parents give each other real nervous looks. I learned more about her over the next few weeks. I found out why they were nervous.

Auntie moved into the extra bedroom—formerly my mom's office—on the first floor. She had it looking good in no time—flowers and little wooden boxes and paintings on the walls. And she put an autographed poster of Jimi Hendrix right over her bed. I thought it looked great, but my parents weren't so sure. They thought she should have moved beyond that stage of her life by now.

But I'd watched her when she thought no one was looking; I'd seen the pain on her face, in her walk. "Why should she grow up?" I said. "She's dying, isn't she?"

School got out for the summer. Mom and Dad were working, and Aunt Wendy and I spent a lot of time together. I went to the clinic with her. They'd given up on the chemo, so all she got there were pain killers and bad news. But she never complained. Instead she just kept telling me stories—about running away from home, from Spokane—when she was eighteen. She went to New York, then California, where she tried singing and modeling and acting, where she joined the peace movement, hanging out with rock bands, where she'd once met Jimi Hendrix and fallen in love with his music. How she kept listening to it when she was older and respectable and selling real estate to blue-haired ladies with poodles. She showed me all her Jimi Hendrix albums, tapes, CDs. She played them for me, sang along, knew every word, knew the exact day he'd died.

I got to like his music, too. Not the way she did, of course. And we *weren't* so much alike after all, I decided, despite my parents' nervousness. I couldn't ever just leave home like she did, talk to my family every few years, see them never. If she hadn't finally decided to call, if my mom hadn't invited her to live with us, she would've been dying alone in some pink stucco building without any family near her. She'd been married twice, she told me, for a total of three years, but she had no kids and no idea of where her ex-husbands were.

"What was it like back then, Auntie?" I asked her once.

"Back in the old days, you mean?" she said.

"When you first went to California. When you traveled around with the bands and went to love-ins and had peace marches and stuff."

"Different from now. Revolutionary ideas everywhere. We had ideals then, and we were determined to carry them out."

My mom had walked into the kitchen where we were sitting and got the milk out of the refrigerator. I could tell she was stalling around, listening, pretending to look through the cupboard for a glass.

"Clean ones in the dishwasher," I told her.

"Right," she said. She poured her milk and left.

"What did you look like then?" I asked Auntie.

"Wait here."

She came back in a minute with an album of pictures. "This is me at a peace rally at Balboa Park in San Diego. Fifty thousand people there that day, and half of them were in the service. The local military authorities weren't amused."

I looked at the picture. I wouldn't have recognized her. She was skinny, with straight blond hair down past her shoulders, beads around her neck, a baggy T-shirt, and navy dungarees that drooped down over her bare feet. The eyes were Auntie's, and the face looked familiar, too. But it was mine. A little older, maybe, but my face, smiling into the camera.

My mom walked back in.

"This one is me at Golden Gate Park," Auntie said. Same girl, same outfit, but her hair was frizzy this time. A guy was standing next to her with his arm around her shoulders. He wore a white T-shirt and jeans, and on his head was a motorcycle helmet with horns. It looked like one of those old Viking hats. His hair was long and blond, and he had this shaggy mustache. He was kind of cute.

"That's Lars," she said. "We met him and his biker buddies at the park. Five hours to L.A. on the back of his Harley that evening. We were flying!" She smiled. "I can still hear the purr of that hog, feel the wind in my face." She spread her knees apart like she was straddling a motorcycle, circled her arms in front of her, leaned her head back, and closed her eyes. Her shorts hiked up on her legs, revealing a tattoo—a blue dove inside a red heart—on the outside of her right thigh.

My mom couldn't take it any longer. She glared at Auntie from across the room. "And what were Lars's ideals, Wendy?" she said. "Was he leading the country toward peace, too?"

Auntie looked at my mom. "Peace?" she said with a grin. "No, Lars wasn't really into peace. He just had this great smile."

My mom frowned. "I'd rather you didn't glamorize your lifestyle to Lisa," she said.

"Lisa's a big girl," Auntie said. "She can see the bad with the good."

"Tell her about both, then."

Auntie got up from the table and headed for the back door. "I'm going to have a cigarette," she said.

"Another thing you shouldn't be modeling for her," my mom said. "And why are you still smoking, anyway?"

Auntie closed the door behind her.

"I'm not going to take up smoking just because I see someone else do it," I told my mom. "I make up my own mind about things."

"I know you do," she said. She went out the back door to where Auntie was standing. I could see them talking; I heard their voices but not the words. Then they were hugging, not letting go, standing and swaying back and forth. I went to my room.

Auntie got home from the clinic one day and told me about a new friend she'd made. This little boy who was being treated for leukemia had adopted her while they were waiting for their appointments. It didn't surprise me—every time we went anywhere, kids would come up and talk to her, hang on her. I don't know what it was. Maybe they could see she was just a bigger kid. Anyway, she'd decided to start doing stuff with the little guy and his mom. They had a movie scheduled for that night.

"It's never too late to be a big sister," Auntie told me.

I saw my mom give her a look and half-open her mouth like she was about to say something. Then she turned away. A few hours later I watched Auntie drive off in Mom's car. I thought she looked like the girl in one of her old pictures again—young, carefree, soft around the edges. Maybe it was just the distance.

She went to see that little boy almost every day. She never invited me to go, and I finally asked her why. She didn't want me to get to know him, she said, in case he didn't get better. She didn't want him leaving a hole in my life. Of course, she always said he was getting better. "I can see it in his eyes," she said.

The eyes were wrong. Her little friend didn't get better. He died.

After Auntie went to the funeral, she was real quiet for several days. When we started talking again, I noticed her eyes had a far-off look in them. I figured she was thinking about her own death creeping up on her. But she wouldn't talk about it.

Auntie did pretty well over the next few weeks: She and I went places, she took walks with my mom every night, cooked a great dinner every couple of days.

"Lisa," she said to me one day, "what do you want to be when you grow up?"

I hate questions like that. Adults only ask them so they can give you *their* opinion afterwards. Plus, I was in a bad mood that day. It was the first time I'd noticed that Auntie didn't seem quite right, that whatever kind of medicine she was on had her under its thumb. I had to admit to myself that her cancer had its ugly foot in the door, that it wasn't going to back off.

"A singer," I said. "No, a model, or an actor, or a hippie, or maybe a groupie. Or how about a real estate saleslady who doesn't know how to use the phone, who lets her niece get to be twelve years old without even knowing her aunt?"

She looked at me for a long time without saying anything. Her smile went away. I felt sick. I wanted my smart-mouth words back, but it was way too late.

Finally she got up from her chair and came around the kitchen table and gave me one of her hugs. But it felt weaker, she felt thinner, and it made me feel worse. "I'm sorry," she said.

"I'm sorry, Auntie," I said, and ran to my room.

The next day we were okay again. She was acting like her old self, making chocolate chip cookies, singing "Purple Haze" as she slid trays in and out of the oven. I wanted her to ask me what I wanted to be when I grew up. I was sure I could think of something. But she didn't ask. I helped her clean up the kitchen, and we walked to the river and sat in the sun and ate warm cookies and got chocolate on our fingers and laughed. She had to stop twice and rest on the walk back home.

August came. Aunt Wendy went to the doctor more often, and she didn't drive anymore. We had to help her into the car, and it hurt me to watch her struggle with it. But she never whined. I wished the doctor could come to see her, but doctors didn't make house calls like they used to, my mom said.

Auntie spent more time on the couch and in her room. A nurse—a crusty little woman named Megan—began coming to the house. I went to the library and read what I could find about cancer. Nothing I learned made me feel better.

I found Auntie standing in front of the bathroom mirror one day. "This rug's gotta go, Lisa," she said, and popped it off. I'd never seen her without the wig, so it was a bit of a shocker. Her hair had come back, at least. It was just that it was short—half an inch long, maybe—and nearly white, and made her look older, almost like a different person. She held the wig out at arm's length and dropped it in the garbage can and smiled into the mirror.

"Now you'll get to know the real me," she said.

That night I stayed up late and took the scissors to my hair until it was practically a crew cut. I kind of liked it, but I knew my mom would hate it. I was ready for her to blow up when she saw me the next morning. Instead, she gave me a big grin.

"At least it's not a tattoo," she said. She went with me to Auntie's room to show her my hair. We all got a big laugh out of it. My mom took a picture of the two of us.

The "real" Auntie stopped eating, got thinner, got dark circles under her eyes, but kept smiling, kept giving hugs. Megan came every day and started giving her food and pain killers through a tube. But Auntie didn't like being in bed. She'd get up every chance she'd get and ask me to go outside with her. She loved sitting in the sun, her face turned up into its warmth.

She'd gone through a lot of changes in a couple of months, but she still liked her music. She still listened to Hendrix and the other sixties stuff whenever she was awake. And she liked me to read to her, which I did whenever she wanted—mostly the tabloids that Megan brought to the house when she was done with them, or new ones that my mom picked up at the store. The headlines were always good for a laugh. And Auntie didn't admit it, but I thought she believed a few of the stories—the tamer ones, anyway.

One afternoon I went in to see her after Megan left. The plastic line dangled down, ending at a needle in her arm. The room smelled sour. I opened the window and a breeze pushed in, billowing out the filmy white curtains my mom had hung, stirring up the pages of the tabloids stacked by the bed. I looked at Auntie. Her eyes were closed, but a Hendrix song was playing real soft on her stereo, and she had this little smile on her face. Maybe she was listening.

Lightning flashed outside the window, followed in an instant by the rumble of thunder. I looked out and saw dark clouds building. The breeze swept across the room again, the pages rustled. One caught my eye. I picked up the paper and glanced at the headline: JIMI HENDRIX'S TWIN WORKING IN SPOKANE GUITAR STORE. I smiled, wondering if Auntie had seen this one. She'd get a big laugh out of it. Maybe if she felt well enough, we could even go to the store and check out the guy. But I looked at her and knew that wasn't real likely. She could still handle her little trips to the backyard, but going downtown would be torture.

Then I got this idea. If she couldn't go there, maybe the guy would be willing to come here. I had some money saved up; I could even pay him. I looked at the name of the paper—*The Inquisitor.* I'd never heard of it. I did know where Gold Strings Music was, though.

As soon as my mom got home, I headed down to the store on my bike. It was raining, but the lightning and thunder had stopped—until I was halfway there, anyway. A big fork of lightning shot down ahead of me—close to downtown—and thunder exploded so loud I could feel it. I sped up, racing through the wet streets.

When I got to the store, it was dark inside. I thought maybe it was closed. But I tried the door any-way, and it opened.

Inside it was real quiet—no music, no people, not even a sales clerk, which I thought was kind of weird. And the only light was coming through the windows. I considered just leaving. I mean, what were the odds of the guy really being there, anyway? But I figured since I'd come this far, I might as well wait and see if some-body showed up.

The door slammed shut behind me. My heart jumped. Nobody was around, but a cold wind blew right past me, chilling the room. I didn't know where that wind had come from—it was warm outside—and it iced my insides and gave me the creeps. I wanted to leave, but something made me stay.

I walked up and down the tall rows of guitars and drums and speakers and sheet music and other stuff, looking to see if anyone was there, listening to my shoes squeak on the old wooden floor. From somewhere I heard a noise, and I stopped in my tracks, in the back corner of the store. It was even darker there, and stuffy and still. I smelled something—a hint of Auntie's perfume or whatever it was she wore. I sniffed my T-shirt, but the scent wasn't there—it was on the air, suddenly moving past me.

I heard the noise again—a guitar playing familiar music. Someone had a Hendrix song on the radio. But the sound tore off in a direction I'd never heard before, building to a wave that came crashing down around my head, and stopped.

A chill ran up and down my backbone. I was afraid to move.

Thunder rolled outside.

I heard the snap of a door latch from the other side, then the sound of someone clearing his throat. I tiptoed to the end of the aisle and looked.

A man was standing behind the counter—a thin black man wearing a red plaid flannel shirt and khaki pants and a smile. Even from across the room I could see the resemblance. It was spooky, but kind of comforting, too—as if I knew him. I walked closer, studying him in the dim light, trying not to stare. But I couldn't help it. It was *his face*—the face on the poster and the album covers.

I bumped into the counter and stopped, three feet away from him. The face still passed the test.

"Can I help you?" he said. The voice was close to the real thing—Jimi Hendrix without music.

"This might sound real dumb, but did you know you're in *The Inquisitor?*"

He nodded, the smile still there. "I wondered when somebody would read the piece and come in. I expected someone older."

I decided to get right to it. "I have a big favor to ask," I said. Then I told him about Aunt Wendy, about her life and her being Jimi Hendrix's number-one fan, and her dying. I told him my idea.

"You want me to impersonate Hendrix—to pretend to your aunt that I'm really him?" The smile was gone. I figured I'd lost him.

"It would mean a lot to her."

"Tomorrow okay?" he said. "I'm off tomorrow."

I couldn't believe it. He was going to do it. I told him yes, tomorrow would be great and gave him directions to the house and said thank you a bunch of times and offered to pay him. But he said he didn't want any money. He'd be there.

The next morning was sunny and mid-August warm. Megan hadn't shown up by nine o'clock, so I unhooked Auntie from her IV myself and got her cleaned up and dressed. She was wide awake—too wide awake, I was afraid—and anxious to get outside. I could see the pain in her face, but she smiled through it. I had her sitting in the backyard sunshine by nine-thirty, listening to me read the paper. The look-alike was due in a half-hour.

She stopped my reading. "Your mom was right, Lisa," she said. "There was bad along with the good."

"I know," I said. "Violence. Drugs and stuff. Mom and Dad filled me in."

At ten he walked around the corner of the house. I couldn't believe it—he'd even gotten himself a cos-tume. He had on this purple tie-dyed T-shirt and black leather bellbottoms and sandals. And strapped across his back was a guitar—a big acoustic one. I was hoping she wouldn't ask him to play it.

She didn't notice him at first—her eyes were closed against the sun. But I had a plan. When he got close, I whipped out a tablet of paper and a pen.

"Mr. Hendrix—Jimi Hendrix!" I said. "Can I have your autograph?" Auntie's eyes snapped open. She stared at him as he took the pen and signed.

He turned to her and smiled. "We've met before, haven't we, Windy?" he said.

She nodded. "Nineteen sixty-nine," she said. "San Francisco."

"I thought so." He took the guitar off his back, tuned it for a moment, pulled a chair up next to her, and sat down. Her eyes were on him the whole time. I held my breath, waiting for her to ask what was going on, who this guy was. But she didn't. I decided the drugs had her believing, or wondering. Or maybe she just wanted to pretend one last time.

He started playing, and he was good. I guess I shouldn't have been surprised—he did work in a guitar store—but he was *very* good. I watched a big smile spread across Auntie's face. Then I went into the house and listened to the music drift in through the open kitchen windows.

He sang to her, and from where I sat it sounded real—softer, slower maybe, but real. I waited for him to stop, to tire of the game, but he kept playing.

It was almost eleven when I glanced at the piece of paper the guy had signed. I hurried to Auntie's room, my breakfast caught in my throat, and looked at her poster. It was the same signature. My heart started pounding. I was on my way outside when the phone rang. Megan was calling to say she was sorry she hadn't made it to the house today or yesterday. I could hear the guitar sounds, the words to "Foxey Lady" through the roar in my ears.

"But I saw you here yesterday," I said. "I talked to you."

"Not me, honey. I'm flat-on-my-back sick. I was too sick yesterday to even call in. But maybe the service sent someone over."

"Maybe," I said, and hung up. The service hadn't sent anyone over. Someone who looked and acted exactly like Megan had been in the house the day before, taking care of Auntie. She'd even brought a fresh supply of tabloids.

The music had stopped. I looked out the kitchen window. He was gone. Auntie was stretched out in her chair, her eyes closed, smiling.

I felt like I was dreaming—nightmaring—but I knew better. I went back to Auntie's room and looked through the stacks of papers. *The Inquisitor* should have been right on top. It was nowhere. I phoned two 7-11s and a PayLess. None of them had ever heard of *The Inquisitor*. I walked outside and sat by Auntie. I held her hand and she said, "Thank you, Lisa," and fell asleep.

I didn't get much rest that night. The next day was Saturday. I got up early and waited around, red-eyed, until I thought the music store would be open, then I headed down there. More lights were on this time, and there were people inside—customers and sales clerks and a guy I figured was the owner. None of them had heard of—much less worked with—anybody like the guy I described to them. They didn't know anything about an article in a paper. They'd closed the store early the day before because of a power failure. No one should have even been in there after four.

None of what they said surprised me, but I didn't want to think about what it meant. I felt haunted.

I went in to see Auntie when I got home. I could tell she was hurting, but she grinned at me from her bed. Her eyes were clear. On the stereo Jimi was singing "The Wind Cries Mary."

"I told your mom about him coming to see me, Lisa," she said. "She patted me on the head. She thinks I've lost it." She laughed softly; the tube leading to her arm quivered.

"I saw him, too," I said. "I heard him. You haven't lost it."

She closed her eyes and settled her head farther into her pillow. The blankets lay almost flat over her wasted body.

I put my hand on hers. It felt cool, dry. "I know what I want to be when I grow up, Auntie," I said.

She smiled. "A groupie?" Her voice sounded dreamy.

"Brave," I said. "I want to be brave."

She fell asleep while I sat with her. She didn't wake up again. Two days later she died.

• • •

It's been awhile now, but I still play her music. I still go by Gold Strings when I'm downtown. If the store is closed and the lights are down, I look through the window, listening for the sounds of a sweet guitar. So far the store's been empty. The only sounds have come from the street, from people passing on the sidewalk. So far.

The Spirit of Franklin Landry

Brosey sat across the kitchen table from Mrs. Caruso, watching the steam rise from her tea, fog her glasses, and soften the deep lines in her face. She'd promised to tell him the story, and he was willing to wait. He needed to know why the old house next door, where he'd lived with his parents for three months now, still gave him the creeps, kept him up at night. She cleared her throat, took a sip, and set down the cup.

"Nineteen-fifty-three, it was," she began. "All in all, things were better then. But there were problems, too. We'd just come out of one war, we were in the middle of another, and some dads were away, some moms were working, some kids were running wild." She frowned, her shoulders slipped a notch lower.

"We'd lived in this house nearly five years when the old lady next door—Mrs. Bono—died. A few months later, Charles Landry and his son, Franklin, moved in. Franklin was twelve, about your age, I'd guess."

Brosey nodded, eager for her to go on.

She did. "Quite the event in this neighborhood."

"Why?" Brosey couldn't picture new people moving in as a big deal.

"They weren't like the rest of the folks around here," she said. "They were colored." Her eyes homed in on Brosey's face.

"Colored?" he said.

"Black," she said. "African-American."

Brosey couldn't recall ever seeing an African-American—or any other minority—in this neighborhood.

"The surprising thing, given the times and all, was that most folks didn't care. Charles Landry was a smart, dignified man, but very friendly, too, and people warmed right up to him. He worked nights as a chemist at the plant. Franklin was a nice boy—small for his age but a hard worker. Took a job delivering newspapers not a month after they moved in. I can still see him struggling with that load of papers on Sunday mornings. In bad weather, his dad would be up helping him, and they'd race each other up the street." She smiled at the memory and then shook her head, the smile fading.

"But things didn't go on good for long. Down the block lived the Cutters. Mr. Cutter was in Korea, Mrs. was waitressing nights, and their two boys—Lane and

Eddie—were having their way with life."

Mrs. Caruso stopped, frowning into her cup, and Brosey glanced at the stove, where the steaming teakettle gave one last meager whistle before going mute. The only sound was the tick of raindrops against the window.

"They were older than Franklin—fourteen and fifteen—and bigger," Mrs. Caruso said, "and mean as neglected dogs. Maybe a month after the Landrys moved in, I saw them chase Franklin down right in front of this house. They dumped his newspapers in the street and started working him over. By the time I got outside, they'd bloodied his nose and ripped his clothes." She shook her head slowly and squinted her eyes.

"Back then an adult's words meant something, and I lit into those two. But they just looked at me, sneers on their faces and hate in their eyes. Then they walked away, slow, swaggering, all giggles and threats.

"I told Mr. Caruso—my husband—about it that night. 'Boys will be boys,' he said. 'Let 'em fight their own battles.' I didn't talk to him for a long while after that."

Brosey leaned closer to Mrs. Caruso, waiting for her to go on.

"I went to their mom first thing the next morning.

Got her out of bed, I did, and she wasn't happy over it. Tried closing the door on me. But I jammed my foot in the door and yelled so she'd have to listen. She opened it back up.

"'They don't belong here,' she said before I could speak. 'That boy got what he deserved. Now get out!' She grabbed the door and pushed it so hard I had to move. It would've broken my foot. I went home angry, but thinking I'd done what I could. I should've done more, I should've gone to the police. But at the time I didn't think they would do anything."

Brosey leaned even closer.

"For the next week, I didn't see or hear anything. I actually thought the Cutter boys had decided to let him be. But one evening my paper didn't come. Right away I got a bad feeling in my stomach. I was standing on the porch, wondering what to do, when I heard shouts. I looked up, and down the street they came, like a fox and two hounds.

"Franklin had shed his papers, and he was flying. The Cutters were struggling to stay with him, huffing and puffing and scowling. Franklin looked confident, like he knew he had them beaten. But I headed for the street just in case. I thought I could slow them down, threaten them, something. Franklin whipped by, flashing me a grin. He cut into his driveway and headed for the house. I stepped in front of the Cutters, but it was like I wasn't there. Lane—the older one—went right through me—knocked me on my rear—and Eddie didn't even slow down to look.

"Franklin had already made it to the porch, and he turned and glared at them before slamming the door behind him. He must've thought he was safe."

"He wasn't?" Brosey asked.

"He must've thought they'd never come into his house after him, because he didn't lock the door. I saw them give each other a look—a real dark look—before they headed inside.

"Franklin's dad wasn't home—his car was gone—so I knew I had to do something. I'd gotten up and started for my house to call the police when the upstairs window flew open and Franklin leaped out on the little roof that covers your porch and front rooms. The Cutters were pushing and shoving and grabbing to be the first to go out the window.

"In an instant they spilled out onto the roof. Franklin had moved to the edge now, but the roof was slick, so they just inched toward him. 'Get off the roof!' I yelled at them, but I might as well have been yelling from the moon. I tried to think of what to do next, but I was frozen—afraid to leave and afraid to stay.

"Franklin had a plan. And my heart about stopped

when I figured out what it was. That apple tree in your yard was a lot smaller then, and its branches were a lot farther from the house—at least ten feet, I'd say. But he glanced at the Cutters one last time and jumped." She squeezed her eyes shut, as if wishing the memory away. Brosey waited, holding his breath.

"He almost made it. He grabbed a branch—a nice, stout one. But he couldn't hold on. He twisted around and fell headfirst and landed in a heap. I ran over to him. I didn't see any blood, but his neck was bent funny. He wasn't breathing. I didn't know what to do except touch his wrist, feel for a pulse. I felt none.

"I looked up at the roof, but the Cutters were gone.

"The ambulance came in a hurry. It didn't matter. The attendants picked up Franklin gently, as if he were still alive, and put him in the back. Then they turned off their flashing lights and drove away. I called Charles at work and told him. Hardest thing I ever did in my life."

Brosey tried to imagine his own parents getting that call. He decided it would break them. "What did he do?"

"He took it real calm. On the phone he said, 'Thank you, Margaret,' after I told him, but before the line went dead I heard a sob. I couldn't get the phone down fast enough.

70

"The Cutters went to trial, if you could call it that. They were considered juveniles—children—so the court gave them children's sentences. The only reason they got any time in detention at all was that Charles wouldn't let up on the prosecutor. And I testified. I told 'em that they'd chased Franklin and beaten him before and that they'd gone after him, right into his house and onto the roof."

Brosey's throat felt dry, but he didn't want to leave the table to get a drink.

"They sent 'em away, but they were home in six months, swaggering down the street and skipping school and bragging to any kid stupid enough to listen. It made everyone in the neighborhood sick, especially Charles.

"After their dad got home, we figured maybe they wouldn't cause more trouble. But little things started happening: Charles would find his tires flat, his mailbox beaten in. Everyone knew who was doing it, but nobody could catch 'em in the act, and their parents wouldn't lift a finger to help."

Mrs. Caruso took a long swallow of tea. "Charles came out one day and found a noose hanging from the tree. He went to the police, but hate crime laws didn't exist back then, and people were just starting to hear about civil rights. The police talked to the Cutters, but they denied everything.

"Months went by, and then one night we woke up to the sound of sirens. My husband and I ran outside, and there was Charles, standing on his front lawn in the light from a burning cross.

"The fire department put out the fire, and the neighbors hauled off the debris. By morning you could barely tell anything had happened. We figured Charles would move, but he wouldn't be run off. He wouldn't leave." She paused for a moment, staring at her cup, giving Brosey a chance to breathe.

"He should have.

"For most of the next year the Cutters were getting in trouble, but the things they were doing—vandalism and shoplifting and fighting—never added up to enough to get 'em locked up for long.

"Then one night Charles told us he'd gotten some threatening phone calls, and he was sure it was the Cutters. They said they were going to kill him if he didn't move out by the next day.

"The police talked to the Cutters, who played dumb, and when nothing happened by the end of the week, everybody kind of let down their guard.

"That Saturday we invited Charles and some other neighbors over for a barbecue. He seemed kind of distant, as if he had a lot on his mind. He went home early. It was the last time we saw him."

Brosey felt his heart pounding, his throat pinching shut. He took a deep breath and waited for her to go on.

"The next afternoon a policeman came to our door, asking if we'd seen Charles. He wasn't home, hadn't been to church, his car was gone. I got nervous right off. Sunday was Charles's day to be home. After church he was always home. Nowhere else.

"That evening the police found his car, driven into the woods off a back road a few miles out of town. They found blood on the back seat, and a ring belonging to one of the Cutters on the front floorboard. Before dark they'd taken the Cutters to jail—they'd been sitting home all innocent-like—and searched their house and yard. They found a bloody baseball bat tucked away in a corner of the garage along with Charles's car keys.

"We were standing out in front of their house with the rest of the neighbors when the police brought the Cutters out, when they carried out that awful bat."

She drained her cup, swallowed hard. "The Cutters did some stupid things when they killed Charles, but the stupidest was waiting. By then, Lane was nineteen, Eddie was eighteen. They weren't juveniles anymore. They got tried as adults and convicted of second-degree murder—they wouldn't ever tell where they'd put the body—but second-degree was enough to put 'em in prison.

"We didn't think the sentence was long enough at the time. But the Cutters didn't do any better in prison than they'd done in the real world. Lane died in a fight less than a year after they went in. A year after that, Eddie got killed in a prison break. So I guess you could say they got life sentences. Or death sentences.

"Some nice people moved into Charles's house after that. They got to be good friends of ours, but I never felt comfortable visiting them. The house never seemed quite right."

Brosey got to his feet without looking up. He'd gotten his story. "I better go," he said.

"Maybe I shouldn't have told you, Brosey."

"I'm glad you did," Brosey managed.

The house felt different when he walked in—just as creepy, but not as puzzling. Mrs. Caruso had undressed the old place, and now he could see its warts. As he hurried up the stairs he thought about Franklin racing up those same steps, the Cutters on his tail. Brosey went to the bedroom and unlatched the window. He tried raising it, but who-knew-how-many coats of paint held it fast. What would Franklin have done if the window hadn't opened? Gone through it? Stood and fought? Stood and fought, Brosey decided. What would have happened then? How would the story have ended?

He took off his shoe and rapped the window's wood frame. He lifted again, and the window rose. A cold blast of wind pushed through the opening, plastering his shirt to his skin, slamming the bedroom door shut. He shivered.

The tree had grown, sent its branches toward the house. Just an easy jump away now, a step. But still, *he* wouldn't do it. The roof was too steep, too slick, and the tree looked scary—gnarled, brittle, bare of leaves or fruit. This was a tree that had once shrugged off a kid and let him drop to his death, a tree whose branches once dangled a hangman's noose. He forced the window back down, lowered the shade, hurried downstairs.

The following Saturday Brosey and his parents cut down the tree. That night the house seemed lighter, warmer, and Brosey slept peacefully for the first time in three months.

The next day, while men came and bulldozed out the stump and hauled everything away, Brosey and his dad drove to the mountains. On a quiet hill behind his uncle's cabin, they found a perfect ten-foot silver fir. That evening they planted it where the apple tree had stood, then leaned on their shovels and admired it in the fading October light. A good replacement, Brosey thought: green and fragrant and new.

Autumn passed and winter arrived and Brosey grew to like the house. The old feelings he'd had all faded away. Or maybe he just got used to them.

Spring came. Brosey saw plants sprout and blossom, watched as bright-green needles—soft as blades of grass—burst out on the branches of the new tree.

One afternoon when he got home from school, he saw a car cruising slowly down the street in his direction. Brosey noticed the license plate was from Oregon. Maybe the driver was lost—this street wasn't a direct route to anywhere. Brosey walked to the curb. Maybe he could help.

The car stopped. Brosey leaned over as the window powered smoothly down.

"Do you live in this house, son?" The driver asked. The voice was deep, young, but Brosey was looking at an old black man, high forehead framed by white hair. His eyes shone bright and brown and friendly above a warm smile. Two little black kids, a boy and a girl— twins, Brosey guessed, seven or eight years old—sat in the back seat.

"This one?" Brosey said, jerking his thumb in the direction of his house.

"Yes."

"Yeah, I—my parents and I—live there."

The old man turned off the car's engine and looked past Brosey at the house.

"Can we get out, Grandpa?" the little girl asked.

"Are you looking for someone?" Brosey asked. "My name's Brosey Kessler. My parents are Douglas and Ellen. Are you looking for us?"

"No, Brosey," the man said, getting out of the car. "I just wanted to see the neighborhood—the house."

"Did you know somebody here?" Brosey asked.

The man closed his door and walked around the car, staring at the house. "My brother," he said finally. "My brother and his son lived in this house."

Brosey stared at the man as he opened the back door and helped his grandkids out of the car. "Charles Landry," Brosey said. "Franklin."

"You've heard the names."

"Mrs. Caruso told me about them."

"Mrs. Caruso." His eyes drifted toward the house next door.

"You want to see the house, Mr., uh, Landry?"

"Would you mind?" he said, moving toward the house, gently guiding the kids across the lawn. They broke loose, chased each other around the fir. "You got rid of the apple tree?"

Brosey nodded.

"Good," the man said. "I never did like that tree."

He stopped at the fir, fingering its moss-green needles, looking it up and down. "I like this puppy, though."

The kids had found a soccer ball and were kicking it back and forth across the lawn. Brosey reached in his pocket. "They can stay out here with me if they want," he said, handing over his house key. "You go in and look around."

"Thanks," Mr. Landry said. "Don't let 'em wear you out."

"Take your time," Brosey said.

"You children mind Mr. Kessler here, okay?" Mr. Landry said. "I'll be right out."

The twins glanced at Brosey and went back to their game. Brosey smiled. Mr. Kessler. He didn't remember being called Mr. Kessler before, even by little kids.

He watched them for a while and then let his eyes wander to the house. A curtain moved in the upstairs window. Mr. Landry's face appeared. He stood looking out for a long time before turning in Brosey's direction.

Brosey pulled his eyes away, feeling like an intruder. He turned back to the kids, but his mind stayed on Mr. Landry.

A few minutes later he came out smiling and handed Brosey the key. "Thanks, Brosey," he said.

"Was it . . . okay?" Brosey said.

"It was fine. Good old feelings. Good new feelings.

Very comfortable." He offered Brosey his hand.

"Thanks again," he said.

Brosey shook his hand, surprised at the old man's strength, at the look in his eye—intense, sad, despite the smile. "No problem," Brosey said, wanting to say more, but Mr. Landry was heading for the car, grandkids on his heels like ducklings.

As Brosey watched him usher the twins into the back seat, he thought suddenly of Mrs. Caruso. He hurried to her front porch.

Mrs. Caruso opened the door, her eyes alight with welcome. "Come on in, Brosey," she said. "Got time for something to drink?"

Brosey glanced over his shoulder. "Someone came," he said. "To the house. Someone came to our house."

"Yes?" she said. "Who, Brosey? Who was it?" Brosey looked over his shoulder again, and her gaze shifted past him, to the street. "Who is it?"

"Mr. Landry's brother came. That's his car on the street."

"Mr. Landry's brother?" she said. She moved onto the porch, grabbed Brosey's elbow. "Hurry, Brosey," she said, turning him toward the street, clinging to his arm as she guided him down the stairs. "Hurry."

They reached the sidewalk. Mr. Landry sat behind the wheel, still studying the house. His head turned.

Mrs. Caruso dragged Brosey a few more feet and stopped.

Mr. Landry's door opened. He got out, eyes on Mrs. Caruso, hands clenching and unclenching at his sides. The back door opened, and the kids joined their grandfather.

Mr. Landry came closer, holding out his hand. "Margaret," he said. "I didn't expect—wasn't prepared—to see you here."

She stood still for a full minute, staring at his face. She reached up and touched his cheek, running her fingers softly over his skin. Her hands went around his back, and they hugged, eyes closed.

"We thought you—" she began, before looking down at the two young faces.

"Things aren't always what they seem, Margaret," Mr. Landry said. "Things aren't always what they seem."

Brosey stared at them. He wanted to ask what was going on, but knew he couldn't. His mind raced, searching for things that might not be what they seemed.

"I'm telling Grandma," the little girl blurted out.

Her grandfather smiled down at her and then laughed, low and long. "I don't think your grandma would mind, Angela," he said finally, stepping back and picking her up in one arm. He draped his other arm around the boy's shoulders. "This is Mrs. Caruso, children—an old friend. Margaret, these are my grand-children, Angela and James."

The girl slid down and stepped forward, shadowed by her brother. Mrs. Caruso bent down and put an arm around each of them, pulling them close. "Beautiful," she said. "Beautiful children."

"A godsend to me, Margaret." He put his hands on their shoulders. "We must go now," he said.

"But where are you?" Mrs. Caruso squinted at his license plate. "Oregon?"

"I know your address," he said. "I'll write to you. As soon as we've both had some time to think about this."

Mr. Landry and the children got into the car. He started the engine, accelerated, left them staring after his tail lights.

Brosey waited for Mrs. Caruso to say something. Her eyes were wide open, but he had a feeling that she wasn't seeing this empty, tree-lined street.

"He'll write," she said finally, still staring off at nothing, speaking to no one.

"He said he would." Brosey's voice was a bare whisper, but it got her attention. She took his arm, and they walked silently back to her door.

"You have baseball now," she said finally, looking at

her watch.

Baseball could wait. "You were friends with this Mr. Landry, too?" Brosey said. "With your neighbor's brother?" Somehow he knew it wasn't the right question, exactly, but he was afraid to ask it any other way.

"Charles Landry didn't have a brother," Mrs. Caruso whispered, as if someone nearby might overhear.

Brosey looked at Mrs. Caruso, hoping for an explanation.

What he got was a smile, a silvery sparkle in her eyes. "Things aren't always what they seem," she said. "Sometimes they're better."

The Slurpers

n his dream, Sidney heard them, up to their usual tricks. Scheming and scuffling. Scraping and scratching. Skulking and skulldugging.

But it wasn't a dream. It never was. He sprang upright in his bed and watched them parade through the tightly latched door, into the dark chill of his room.

Between his fingers, through the narrowest of spaces, he counted them. One. Two. Three. Always the three, the same three, drifting slowly toward him.

In the light from the street lamp on the corner—a glimmer that barely sifted through the curtains—their eyes glowed green, then yellow, then red. Their mouths, even in the darkness of his room, were black holes, smiling swampy smiles. And inside those black holes, Sidney saw rows of jagged crocodile teeth the color of wet moss.

He yanked the blankets over his head and fell back, flattening himself against his mattress, squeezing his eyes shut.

He heard his heart thumping, a bass drum somewhere beneath his trembling, and he heard *them*, too.

Slinking and slithering. And slobbering and slurping. Always the slushy sound of slurping.

They were gathered around his bed now, close enough that he could smell them.

"Dad!" he yelled from underneath his sheet. But his dad didn't answer. "Mom!" he screamed. His mom didn't come.

And still he heard them. Besieging and bedeviling. Mumbo-ing and jumbo-ing. And slurping. Always slurping.

He had to make a run for it. Through squinted eyelids he peeked, looking for an escape route. To the left of him, eyes. To the right of him, eyes. And directly above him, hovering near the ceiling, more eyes.

But straight ahead lay a clear path to the door. He threw off his covers, leaped, and hit the floor running, eyes wide open now, searching for the doorknob. Behind him, he heard the slurping—suddenly louder, angrier.

His outstretched hand hit the wall, then the bookcase, and finally, just as he felt their hot breath on his neck, the door—and the doorknob.

He twisted and pulled and flew from the room, churning up the hallway to his parents' bedroom. Without looking back, he burst in and launched himself onto their bed.

"The Slurpers!" he screamed. "They're here again!"

"Again?" his dad mumbled, pulling his pillow over his head. "The surfers?"

"Not in Iowa, Sid," his mom said, pushing herself up on one elbow.

"No!" Sidney yelled. "Slurpers!" He wedged himself between them. "In my room! Again!"

"Oh . . . yeah," his dad said. "Slurpers. I thought we got rid of 'em last time."

"You didn't."

"You stay here with your mom. I'll go roust 'em out."

A minute later he was back. "All gone," he said.

"I'm staying here," Sidney said.

"You could try thinking only good thoughts," his mom said. "Then you'd have only good dreams."

"Like your birthday," his dad said. "You could think about your birthday party."

"They're not dreams," Sidney said, "and I'm staying here."

"Your choice," his dad said, and crawled in next to him.

Sidney took a deep breath and relaxed. It felt good to be sandwiched between his mom and dad, where the Slurpers wouldn't come.

He closed his eyes and slept.

The next morning he woke up all alone in the big

bed. He thought about his birthday, and he smelled something good baking. His mom was making his cake.

He raced downstairs. The cake was out of the oven and looking perfect. And his dad had gotten a good start on the decorations. Sidney looked at the clock.

Eleven! He had never slept this late.

"Tired, birthday boy?" his dad said.

"Not now," Sidney said. But he must have been tired last night. Now there were only three hours to go until his party.

The time hurried by, and then the magic hour arrived. Just after the last of his friends had come, the doorbell rang once more. For a moment, Sidney felt a tickle of fear running down his back. But the Slurpers wouldn't come in the daylight. And they sure wouldn't ring the doorbell.

"Why don't you get it, Sid," his mom said.

Sidney opened the door and jumped back. A clown stood on the doorstep—on his head. The funniest-looking clown Sidney'd ever seen. Except for his bright white face, he was all green—hair, hat, shoes, clothes, even his nose. He flipped back onto his feet and smiled a smile that spread from ear to ear.

"You Sidney?" he said, pinning a saucer-sized green plastic flower on Sidney's shirt.

Sidney nodded.

"I'm Yendis," he said. "Yendis the clown." He strolled in, and the party started.

Yendis *was* the party. He organized the games and performed fantastic magic tricks and made balloon hats for everyone. He even cut the cake and scooped the ice cream.

While they were eating, Sidney's friends got a little wild. Michael McDougall's hat got popped by a stray fork. Sidney watched Michael fight back tears—the hat had been an excellent one, and Yendis was out of balloons.

So Sidney gave him his own hat—a swashbuckling thing made of purple and yellow and white balloons that would have made any pirate proud. Michael's smile was worth more than the hat. And Sidney was a year older now. He could do that older kind of stuff.

Finally it was time for the party to end—time for Yendis to go. He stood by the door and tenderly shook the hands of Sidney's friends as they left, until only Sidney and his mom and dad were standing with him. And Sidney didn't want it to be over.

"Did you make a good birthday wish, Sidney?" Yendis said.

"Yes," Sidney said. He had made a very good birthday wish.

"Do you wish it to come true?"

"Yes," Sidney said. He very much wished it to come true.

"Then you must do a favor for me," Yendis said, opening up his old cloth duffel and digging through it. "When you go to bed tonight, you must wear these." He held out a green wig and a green nose just like the ones he wore. "These are for you to keep. To pass on someday."

Sidney looked at his mom and dad, but they were staring at each other, their faces filled with questions.

Yendis put the nose on Sidney's nose and the wig on Sidney's head. He shook hands with Sidney's dad, bowed to his mom. Then he squatted down and gave Sidney a giant hug.

"You're a very special boy, Sidney," he said. "I'd like to visit you again sometime." He was out the door before Sidney could say good-bye and nowhere in sight by the time Sidney looked out the window.

That night Sidney headed to bed early, wearing his green hair and green nose. He liked his looks in the mirror—kind of like a miniature Yendis, he thought.

"Night-light on, Sid?" his dad said. He always asked, even though Sidney had never said no.

Sidney thought a moment, recalling his reflection. "Not tonight, Dad."

His dad looked at him and then bent and kissed him, smiling at Sidney's funny face. "Okay," he said.

"But come and get us if you change your mind."

He didn't change his mind. He lay in his bed in the dark, picturing how his nose looked, and feeling the warmth of the fuzzy wig. He fell asleep wondering how Yendis had known his wish.

A scuffling sound woke him. Then the scraping. And slurping. He heard them slither through the door, but he didn't hide. He sat up in bed, a smile on his face, and watched them come.

They saw him and stopped, hanging in the air, looking like mildewed laundry. Their grinning faces froze. Their eyes stared and then blinked, and their lips began to move. They were mumbling now and whispering—frightened, quavery whispering.

Suddenly they whirled frantically around in a circle and then spun off one by one to race through the room, searching for something. But they stayed far away from Sidney's bed, not even daring to look, not even daring to slurp.

They came together in the center of the room, a throbbing knot of nervous bewitchment. They stole glances in Sidney's direction and murmured among themselves like the pieces of a broken heart.

Sidney stared back. He wanted them out of his room—out of his life—now. He planted his feet on the floor and stood tall. Across the room, he saw himself in his dresser mirror—big green nose and frizzy green hair—and stretched himself even taller, until his bones creaked. The Slurpers shrank back, ugly heads turned away.

Arms outstretched, teeth bared, he took a giant step—right at them. They screeched, flew away, rocketing toward the door. They were gone, leaving only the faint smell of something moldy. Sidney stood, arms folded, a smile spreading wide under his big green nose.

The light filtering in through his window flickered, and he turned toward it. Outside, the streetlight brightened, its lamp suddenly ablaze. On the sidewalk, nearly hidden in the shadow of a big maple tree, stood a solitary figure, looking up at Sidney's bedroom window. Sidney knew instantly who it was. The wig and nose and clothes were black—not green—in the lamplight, but he knew.

Sidney raised his hand and waved, and Yendis waved back. He flashed Sidney the thumbs-up sign and then bowed deeply as the streetlight flared brighter. Then suddenly it went dark, hiding him under a blanket of moonless sky.

Breathless, Sidney waited, but Yendis—for tonight, anyway—had disappeared. Sidney turned reluctantly from the window and glanced around the room. Still empty. Slowly he removed the nose and wig, stuffing them gently into his pajama bag.

He crawled into bed. The Slurpers wouldn't be back, he thought. But as he lay under his covers, warm and snug, he reached out a hand and touched the bag. He pulled it close—just in case—and fell asleep.

Shadow Canyon

saac hit the uphill and shortened his stride, head down, concentrating on his breathing. A half-mile ahead, just beyond the Entering Waterville sign, the hill crested. From there, it was another half-mile to the high school, where he'd do forty minutes of interval work before the three-mile run back home.

Something moved off to his right, at the edge of the field. In the dim light it was simply a shadow rising from the stubble. Startled, he jumped, throwing himself off stride. A deer, probably. He'd seen plenty of them in the daylight, or when he was riding around with his mom after dark.

He got back on pace, eyes on the road, on the vague, pre-dawn outline of the town closing in up ahead. But he still sensed movement in the field—something keeping up with him. He glanced right, unconsciously slowing, but saw nothing through the murk. A dog, maybe. Some black farm dog out on a chicken raid.

He slowed to a stop, listening. For a moment he held his breath, stared into the field. Nothing. He exhaled silently. The only sound came from his heart, thumping like a machine gun. And then something else: the crack of dry wheat stubble underfoot. A deer after all, he decided.

His legs felt tight when he started off again. He'd passed the first unlighted buildings before his breathing fell into a rhythm with his feet.

His morning ritual hadn't changed since he'd moved here from Seattle—two hundred miles and fifty years away—in June. Six days a week he ran. On Saturdays—his day off—he got on his bike and rode vacant highways and dirt roads and livestock trails. The work kept him in shape and filled the empty hours and took his mind off the divorce. And he got to see the countryside: sleepy, rough-edged towns; oceans of grain surrounding islands of houses and buildings and shade trees; the Columbia River, a giant blue reptile snaking through brown desert; valleys carved by ancient ice fields; a huge empty sky stretching above him in all directions. But this morning, he couldn't see much beyond his next footfall. October had arrived. The days had grown short.

Soon he was striding through the parking lot under ghostlike lights, heading past the brick buildings. The cinder track lay behind the school. Beyond the track, he could just make out the end of the school grounds, the start of the hills rolling off to the south. He jogged to a stop and checked his watch. He'd made it in just under eighteen minutes, even with the distraction— the deer. Not bad for a training run. He reset his watch and moved to the inside lane.

His workouts were tougher than the ones he had with his cross-country team. And the work had paid off. So far he was undefeated, untouched in dual meets, which was unheard of in a freshman, even in the small-school classification where he was competing. He wondered sometimes how he'd do against the big-school guys. When he got the big city newspapers, he compared times. He decided he'd be doing well. He just hoped that someone who mattered would be paying attention.

He had to get to the invitational. He had to. And his coach told him it was possible, if he kept working. One other runner from Waterville had made it, he'd said.

He was halfway through his third 400, moving smoothly up the backstretch, when he heard someone behind him—breathing, footsteps. At first he thought—hoped—he was imagining it. But he knew better. He headed into the curve, hugging the inside lane, trying to stay calm, loose. Maybe he'd inspired one of the other guys on his team. They all knew about his workouts. So far they'd chosen not to join him, but maybe today was the day. Isaac had a feeling that it wasn't.

Halfway through the turn, the runner pulled even with him, just off his shoulder, and held the pace. "Morning," he grunted.

Isaac glanced over. "Morning," he said, eyes back on the track.

"Mind if I join you?"

"No," Isaac said. The kid could join him for an interval or two, and then Isaac would leave him in his dust. Isaac picked up the pace as they hit the straight-away; the guy matched him stride for stride. Isaac backed off to a jog at the bleachers, checked his watch. Sixty seconds flat. A little fast.

"Another four next?" The guy had turned toward Isaac and was backpedalling up the track a few feet ahead, waiting, smiling. He was about Isaac's height, 5'7" or 5'8", but broader across the shoulders, thicker through the chest, older. Isaac guessed he was probably a couple years out of high school.

"Yeah," Isaac said. "And then four threes and four twos."

"Great," the guy said, falling in beside Isaac.

"And I've already done three miles on the road, and some eights and sixes."

"Super. You on the cross-country team?"

"Yeah." Did this guy think Isaac was just out here for his health?

"Having a good year?"

"Undefeated."

"I bet you are."

They finished the lap in silence. Isaac set his watch and took off, the guy on his right shoulder, step for step. He told himself not to press, to relax, to stay loose, but he knew he was pushing it. They moved through the curve and into the backstretch, and Isaac listened for the other runner's breathing, but he barely heard him. Maybe he wasn't going to blow this guy away. Maybe this farm boy could run.

Isaac checked his watch at the finish— :58.3. Faster than he ever ran these things in practice, and he could feel it. "Good pace," he said, setting off on his warm-down lap. The other runner turned and jogged in place, waiting, his grin friendly below dark, sparkling eyes and straight, sandy hair. In the first light of morning, Isaac could make out a faded Oregon T-shirt, yellow with green letters, raggedy cut-off gray sweats, and beat-up white Adidas low-cuts—funny-looking leather shoes with green stripes. They looked familiar—something he'd seen in his dad's old college pictures, maybe.

"Wanna buy my shoes?" The guy's laugh echoed off

the buildings—a rich, bright laugh, edged with mis-
chief.

"Trade you," Isaac said, laughing himself and then
suddenly praying that his offer wouldn't be taken ser-
iously. He was wearing hundred-dollar Nike trainers.

"Can't," the guy said. "Good-luck shoes."

Isaac relaxed, getting his breath back, striding up
the backstretch.

"What's your name?" the guy said.

"Isaac. Yours?"

"Danny."

They finished the lap and ran the first of the 300s.
Isaac gave up on the idea of leaving Danny in his dust.
He wasn't sure why he'd wanted to. "You live around
here?" he asked on the next breather lap.

"Not far." Danny gestured toward the hills. So—he
really was a farm boy. "You?"

"Three miles. My mom's a doctor here now."

"Your dad?"

"Seattle. With his new wife."

"Tough, huh?"

"Yeah." It was tough. It was tough being away from
his dad, from his friends. Tough going into exile just so
his mom could make a fresh start. A clean break, she
said, from the rat race, the old way of life.

Isaac didn't want a clean break. But he didn't want

to talk about it, either. "You in college?"

"Taking some time off."

"Must be nice."

Danny didn't answer. They jogged to the start of the 300. "Boom," Danny said and laughed, and they shot off down the backstretch.

Isaac felt the pace in his legs, in his lungs, in his gut. But he glanced over and saw a smile. Danny had to be working—a line of sweat inched down his temple—but he was enjoying himself. Isaac pushed down the urge to back off, to let him go. He could hang in with him. He knew he could.

They finished together, started their jog lap. "How old are you?" Danny said.

"Fourteen." But Isaac suddenly felt older. His legs were heavy; his chest ached.

"Fourteen?" Danny said. For a moment he said nothing. "A freshman?"

Isaac nodded, saving his breath.

"You're good, Isaac," Danny said finally. "You're very good."

"Thanks," Isaac managed. "But not as good as you."

"I've got a lot of years on you."

Isaac's breathing was coming easier. "You think you could help me out?" he said. "With my workouts, I mean? If you're going to be around for a while, that is."

"You're doing fine on your own."

"I could do better."

They finished the next curve. "You've got a goal?"

Isaac didn't answer for a moment. He felt foolish—naïve—just talking about it. "The invitational," he said finally. He waited for Danny to laugh.

"The invitational," Danny said. A smile, not a laugh. "Perfect. A perfect goal."

"You think so?"

"Perfect. Tough, but within your reach. And if you don't make it this year, you've got three more chances."

"I need to make it this year." They jogged into the curve.

"Why? You quitting school after this year?"

"So my dad can see me run," Isaac said after another dozen steps. He felt as if there were more than two hundred miles separating him and his dad already. What would the distance be by the next year, or the year after? He needed to get his dad's attention soon, before he forgot he ever had a son.

"He doesn't come over to any of your meets?"

"It's a long drive."

"Yeah." Danny stopped at the starting line and spit into the grass.

"So you'll help me out?" Isaac looked at Danny's face for an answer.

"I'm not a coach," Danny said. "But sure, if you want the help, I'll do it."

Isaac did want the help. He knew he had to get better. "Good," he said.

"Good." Danny smiled and pointed his finger—the barrel of a gun—at the sky. "Boom." They took off, quicker this time, and Isaac could feel his breath coming harder. What had he gotten himself into?

The next morning he arrived at the track early; Danny was already there. They stuck with the basics of Isaac's routine, but the intervals were more intense, and before every recovery lap, they ran ten sets of bleacher stairs, high-stepping up, bounding down. On the run home, Isaac pushed himself. He couldn't give back what he'd gained in the workout. He had it in the bank, now; it had to stay there.

The next day was the same, and the next, but on Friday they backed off. "You've got a meet tomorrow," Danny said. "We need to get you faster, but you also need to get noticed. That's not gonna happen if you run a race with dead legs." He looked at Isaac and smiled. "But we'll make up for it Sunday."

Isaac ran a strong race: He beat the second-place guy by thirty-seven seconds. So when he and Danny met at the track on Sunday morning—in the dark and cold and wind—and just followed their usual routine,

Isaac figured maybe Danny was rewarding him for his victory.

"Tomorrow," Isaac grunted at the end of the last warm-down lap. He turned and started for home.

"We're not done yet." Danny was heading across the football field toward the backstretch when Isaac turned. "Come on!" he yelled.

By the time they hit the first field of stubbled wheat, they were running shoulder to shoulder. They angled right, not talking, moving fast. The dirt felt good under Isaac's feet, the air felt good in his lungs, and he was ready for anything.

They moved over one gentle hill and another, running straight across fields, crossing a dirt tractor road. Ahead the terrain looked flat, unchanged, unchallenging, but Danny wasn't just running; he was going somewhere.

A gust of cold wind whipped across the fields, bringing water to Isaac's eyes, but through the tears, through the gray light, he saw a dark line appear on the horizon. Some kind of mirage, he figured, but it put an edge on the flat surface of this world. He kept his eyes on the line as they got closer. It thickened, gaining depth.

Danny must have seen the question on his face. "The canyon," he said.

"What canyon?"

"You'll see. We're gonna run its wall."

They pushed up a low hill, hitting its crest together. "There," Danny said. From the top of the rise, Isaac could look across the rolling countryside. It continued on in all directions, except straight ahead. Straight ahead—less than a mile away, he figured—it ended, dropping off into a dark hole.

Isaac felt his stomach knot up. Run its wall? What did that mean? Something exciting, he told himself. Something fun. No reason to be scared. He spit on the dirt and picked up the pace, and Danny matched him, laughing.

They approached the canyon, angling toward its north rim, and Isaac watched it open up, its edges soften. "How'd it get here?"

"Glacier," Danny said. "They think a big chunk got pushed up in here."

"What happened to it?"

"Melted. Soaked in. Evaporated. Nothing left but this big hole. The canyon."

They hit a narrow trail and followed it toward the canyon edge. The ground tilted away, gradually at first, and then steeply, until the path dropped below the rim of the canyon. To Isaac's right, a wall of rock rose toward gray sky. To his left, a couple of feet of path, and a dropoff, and thin air, and the south wall of the canyon in the distance.

He glued his eyes to the rocky path and Danny's feet in front of him. He figured the canyon floor lay two hundred feet below the rim. The trail was taking them down in a hurry, but they were nowhere close to halfway down yet. He moved closer to the wall.

The trail switched back sharply, and suddenly they were heading east, the wall on their left, the abyss on their right. Isaac glanced down and spotted a narrow streak of black at the very bottom of the canyon, running along most of its length. Water had seeped in here from somewhere.

The trail levelled off and merged into the canyon floor. They were down, running toward the other end. "Quick tour," Danny grunted over his shoulder.

Isaac glanced around. Above them, the sky was growing brighter, but here everything was shadow and silence. He heard breathing and footfalls and nothing else. It was as if light—and life—in this giant hole existed in a different time zone.

They reached the strip of water and skirted its east bank. Fifty feet from the canyon's south wall, Danny cut to his right to head back the other side. Off to the left a trail zig-zagged up the cliff. "Why don't we go up here?" Isaac said.

They'd made the turn and were heading back before

Danny answered. "I don't go that way," he said. "And if you ever come here alone, you don't go that way."

Once they'd started up the trail, Isaac's legs felt as if they were churning through quicksand. Up ahead, Danny had slowed, too. Head down, arms pumping, he was grinding it out, his old shoes digging into the incline.

They'd barely reached the top when Danny turned and started down again. By the time they got to the bottom, Isaac could breathe, but without a word, without a glance, Danny headed up again. Was he trying to kill them? Isaac felt half-dead already. But he fell in behind Danny. He wasn't going to quit.

They reached the canyon rim, and then it was down, and up, and down again. At the end of their fifth ascent, Danny jogged to a stop and bent over, hands on his knees. Isaac followed his example, but he felt like lying down, vomiting. He took a deep breath and let it out; it sounded like a moan, a cry for help.

"You praying?" Danny said.

"Dying man's prayer."

"Save it for the real thing," Danny said.

The real thing? Did he mean dying?

"You seen the course?" Danny asked him.

"I know where it is—out in the Snohomish Valley—but I don't know the course."

"There's a section coming up out of the valley about halfway into the race. It's as steep as this trail but longer, and it'll eat you up if you're not ready for it." He took a deep breath and straightened up. "If you let it take away your rhythm, you'll never get it back. You'll lose the race right there."

Isaac didn't doubt it. Five times up the trail had taken all the starch out of him. He couldn't imagine running another three miles at race pace.

"Tomorrow we'll do six down-and-backs, then seven," Danny said. "We'll get to ten and hold, working on times. You've got a month to get ready."

A month to get ready—if he got an invitation. Danny seemed to take it for granted; Isaac didn't. He stood up. His lungs weren't complaining as much, his heart had slowed to a double-time jackhammer beat. "Let's go to ten tomorrow," he said.

A grin lifted one corner of Danny's mouth. "Tomorrow it is, Boy Wonder."

They turned their backs on the canyon and jogged off on the trail. Danny stopped at the first dirt road. "I'm heading back," he said. "You can follow this road to the highway—about a mile, probably—and take a left. You'll be nearly home."

Isaac started down one of the wheel ruts. "See you tomorrow," he called out, glancing back.

"Tomorrow," Danny said.

Isaac saw him accelerate across the field, shoes moving like pistons, until he disappeared over the hill.

That week he got another first place, despite legs that felt lead-heavy. Ten trips a day up the wall of the canyon were leaving their mark. The following week he took another first, this time by over a minute.

On Tuesday of the next week, Coach Harrell called Isaac into his office. He tossed an envelope across the desk. "Sit down, Isaac," he said with a smile, "and open your mail."

Your mail. Isaac ripped open the envelope. They wanted him to run in the invitational. He felt himself floating, drifting up from the chair, barely aware that his legs were lifting him. "Yes!" he said, pumping his fist in the air.

"I could say it was coaching, but you've got your own motivation, don't you?"

"I guess. But I couldn't have done it without you. And Danny."

"Danny," the coach said. "An older brother or something?"

"An older guy. A good runner. The best I've seen. Runs me into the ground. Runs me till I want to quit. But I don't."

The coach leaned forward, hands twisted together

in front of him. "Seattle guy?" he said. The smile was still there, but it looked plastered on.

"Local."

"Last name?"

"Don't know. You know him?" He probably did. He'd probably coached him. Unless Danny'd moved here after high school, the coach had to know him.

"What's he look like?" the coach had gotten up from his chair and was pacing around the small room. Isaac described Danny to the coach, told him how they'd met, what their routine had been over the past few weeks.

The coach sat back down and turned toward the window. Isaac couldn't see his face, but the back of his neck below the gray hair had lost its color. Finally he pivoted around and faced Isaac. "Don't know him." He forced a smile. "For a minute, I thought I might. But he sounds like an excellent coach. He must think a lot of you."

"He's helped a lot."

"Will he make it to any of your meets?"

"He seems pretty busy."

"Uh-huh." The coach got up. "Anyway, Isaac, congratulations."

Isaac took his hand. It felt cold and damp, and for a second Isaac could feel it tremble. But the coach squeezed down until his grip steadied, until Isaac's hand ached, and then he let go, forcing one last smile on Isaac.

"Keep after it," he said.

"I will." Isaac turned to go.

"I know. But be careful. And stay off the south wall."

The south wall again. Danny must've been right. But how bad could it be?

When he saw Danny the next morning, Isaac didn't say anything about the invitational. But even in the dark, it must've shown on his face.

"You did it, didn't you," Danny said on their first lap around the track.

"Yeah," Isaac said, trying to sound nonchalant.

Danny's teeth flashed white in the dim light from a distant lamp. "Way to go, Boy Wonder," he said. "But you know what this means."

Isaac didn't know, but he had an idea. "What?"

"You've gotta work harder."

Isaac spit on the grass. He didn't care if he had to work harder. "Okay."

"Just going ain't good enough. You want to do well, you want to win."

"I'm only a freshman."

"Doesn't matter. That just means you've got

nothing to lose. It means you're gonna make those other guys nervous."

They finished the lap. "They won't even know who I am," Isaac said.

"They'll pretend they don't, but they'll know. The guys that don't talk to you before the race are the nervous ones—the ones who've been thinking about you the most. They'll be looking over their shoulders, waiting for you to run up their backs."

Maybe Danny was right. "How will I run up their backs when I'm in front of 'em?"

Danny smiled over at him. "Good attitude, Boy Wonder," he said.

● ● ●

The first Saturday in November—race day—finally arrived. Isaac was still unbeaten, unchallenged, and he felt strong. They'd tapered his training for the past week—on Wednesday and Thursday they confined their workouts to the track—but on Friday they ran, slow and silent, to the canyon. Instead of heading down to the floor, Danny led Isaac on a ragged route around the canyon rim. Above the south wall they cut close to the edge, and in the fading moonlight, Isaac saw the beginnings of a trail down. But they didn't take it. The wall looked steep and ugly and forbidding, and he saw the shine of ice on the rocks. But he knew that if Danny had started down, he would have followed him.

They stopped at the top of the north trail. Isaac was hoping Danny would give him some good news—that he'd be going to the race. Instead, Danny stared out at the canyon before looking Isaac in the eye. "Your next meet's for real," he said. "Remember, you deserve to be there just as much as anyone. Hold your head up. Show 'em you belong. During the race—especially on the pipeline hill—keep your head up. It'll help you stay on pace. And after the race, guess what?"

"Head up," Isaac said.

"No matter what happens."

"Okay."

"And if your dad doesn't show, run for yourself. Run for yourself anyway. Run for me." He gave Isaac a thumbs-up sign and began jogging backwards the way they'd come. "Go get 'em, Boy Wonder!" he said. He gave Isaac one last grin and took off striding, and then sprinting, across the field.

Isaac opened his eyes to the gray light seeping into the car. His mom had turned into a long driveway that ran past a neat yellow farmhouse to a fenced pasture. Beyond several rows of parked cars, a crowd of people stood, milling around. Among the crowd he saw other runners, set off by their colorful warmups, their nervous pacing, their stretching and bouncing. Isaac's mom pulled into a spot and turned off the engine. Sweat crept from his armpits. He heard music—soft wisps of music from an old movie he'd watched with his dad a long time ago. A movie about Olympic runners. "Did you call and remind him?" he said.

"Yes," his mom said. "He sounded excited. Said he'd be here."

He didn't see his dad's car. But it was early—forty-five minutes till the ten-o'clock start. "I'm gonna go check in, Mom." He needed to get some blood moving. The half-hour drive from the hotel—and the four-hour trip yesterday—had left him feeling logy.

"Okay, honey." She put her hand on his head, tousling his hair. "I'll see you at the start. And the finish. Good luck."

Forty minutes later, he'd talked to no one except the officials. Danny'd been right—the other runners were trying to ignore him. He recognized a couple—Coats from Roosevelt, and Stull, the hometown favorite from Snohomish. Both of them already had four-year scholarships to colleges the next year. But he caught them glancing at him, and then glancing away. Thinking about him.

A group had gathered at the start, moving around,

eyeing positions. Before Isaac reached the line, a tall guy—dark hair, smile, Mead High School warmups—approached him and held out his hand. Isaac knew him—Jason Burke, last year's big-school cross-country champ, winner of the 1600 and 3200 at the state track meet.

"Isaac, right?" he said. The smile looked real.

"Right," Isaac said, taking his hand. "You're Jason? I've heard a lot about you."

"I've heard a lot about you, too," Jason said. "Good luck."

"You, too." Isaac looked at his watch. It was time. And now the butterflies—the same ones that worked his insides before every race—were back, but there were more of them. He shed his warmups, gave them to his mom, and jogged to the start—far left, he decided, away from the crowd. He still hadn't seen his dad. But Isaac had paid the price to get here; he wasn't going to throw away the weeks of work and pain he'd invested. He'd do his best to run—and win—for himself.

The gun exploded. He took off, head up, hands down, fighting to keep loose. The pace was fast, but he couldn't let himself get buried at the start. He saw three guys pulling ahead, but all the other runners—more than fifty guys and girls—were bunched, heading across a flat field of chalk-lined grass toward the hills in the distance. A hundred meters ahead of them stood a white fence with an open gate in the middle and a dirt road beyond. The opening looked wide—big enough for cars to drive through—but a bottleneck if everyone stayed this close. He accelerated, drifted right, falling in behind the three leaders—Burke and Coats and Stull. Everyone else was behind him now, and the crowd of spectators on either side was thinning out. He glanced around, searching for his dad, but the faces were a blur. He concentrated on the leaders, ten meters ahead and running elbow to elbow. He couldn't just rely on them burning themselves out. What if they didn't? This was a long race by cross-country standards—a 10K—but if he let them get away, he might not catch them.

The first kilometer ticked by—flat, winding, country road—and Isaac got into a rhythm. The air was cool and damp—no wind, no rain—and he felt good, but he held himself back. Still a long way to go. Still the hill. They passed the 2K marker— an official barking out times, another with a clipboard, a few spectators. None was his dad. He decided to quit looking.

The road crossed a river on a low bridge. He glanced over his shoulder at the runners stringing out behind him, dropping back. A paved trail followed the river north. Four hundred meters later the river elbowed, heading toward the hills. He was hanging in there—

he'd seen Coats and Stull both look back, checking on him. Burke's head never moved.

At the 3K mark, the course left the river, continuing along another country road. Then it left the road, heading straight across a flat field toward a low, solitary hill.

The course started up the hill on a narrow dirt path that cut between trees and undergrowth—an easy incline. Without trying, Isaac gained a few meters on the guys in front of him, who were now running single file, Burke in the lead.

They crested the hill and started down. Through the trees, Isaac could see a flat field in front of them, and then more hills, rising up dark green. He looked for the pipeline trail—a vertical slash on the side of the hill, Danny had told him—but he couldn't see it.

They passed the 5K mark—a couple of officials, a handful of spectators—and continued along the trail. They were halfway there. Isaac still hadn't seen the hill, but they were running in the shadow of the hills now, and he knew it was close.

Another kilometer of flat terrain took them to an official planted in the middle of the trail, with his arm pointed toward the hills. This was it—the pipeline. Isaac blinked the sweat out of his eyes and let his arms dangle for a moment. He had to stay loose.

Burke took the turn, then Coats and Stull running stride for stride. Isaac was next, five meters behind. He hit the gravel and looked ahead—and up. A hundred meters away, the hill rose like a fortress wall, the pipeline trail cut straight up its side.

Isaac remembered what Danny had told him—keep your head up, keep your stride consistent, keep loose. He lifted his head, took a deep, deep breath, and locked himself into a stride.

The hill came on fast. One moment he was running, strong and smooth, on the flat. The next, he felt as if a big hand had grabbed him around the chest and squeezed. He remembered what Danny had told him about the canyon. This wasn't steeper. It wasn't. But he looked up to where the gravel trail met gray sky, and it was like lying on his back and staring at a cloud. How far was it?

His heart thumped louder now, his breathing was harsh and labored, and his legs felt as if he were knee-deep in mud. He watched the backs of the other runners, focused on something besides his own pain. Burke was still ten meters ahead, Coats five. Stull had slipped back a step. He was in third now, four meters in front of Isaac, and then three, and two and one, and Isaac was on his shoulder, chugging past him, looking ahead, looking up. He kept his knees lifting, kept moving, and stayed close to Burke and Coats.

The hill drifted past inch by painful inch, until a quarter of it remained. And suddenly Coats was in trouble. He stumbled and staggered and slowed, and Isaac rolled by him like a freight train.

Still ahead of him was Burke, who reached the crest of the hill and went over the top. For a moment Isaac lost sight of him, for a moment he panicked. Then he topped the hill himself and saw an official straight ahead, and Burke disappearing into the trees to the right. The official pointed after Burke, and Isaac followed, trying to catch his breath and regain his stride. But the hill had taken it out of him. He looked ahead, down the narrow, dark, tree-lined path, and saw Burke slowly pulling away. And there wasn't anything Isaac could do about it. He felt heavy-legged and light-headed, and everything shifted to slow motion: his stride, his breathing, the trees and bushes floating by on either side.

And the clapping. From somewhere he heard the sound of clapping. He glanced around, saw nothing at first. But just ahead, ten meters to the left of the path, the trees thinned out into a clearing. And in the clearing a shadowy figure stood, looking out at Isaac—and clapping in slow motion, smiling. Danny had come after all.

"All downhill from here, Boy Wonder," he said. "You can catch him." He gave Isaac the thumbs-up sign, and then Isaac was past him. He glanced back, but his eyes blurred over with tears and sweat, and he lost sight of Danny. He had to get moving. He had to catch Burke. Suddenly his legs felt loose again, strong, his breathing was coming easier. He accelerated, his eyes fixed on Burke's back.

The trail continued along the crest of the hill and then started down. He caught Burke there, right at the 7K sign, where a group of people gave them both a hand, shouted encouragement. Then they were on their own, running shoulder to shoulder downhill and onto the flat, past the 8K mark, along roads and trails, and across fields. Wordless, neither giving an inch, they hit 9K, running along the shoulder of a country road, approaching the farmhouse where the race had begun. Spectators lined both sides of the pavement, but their faces were out of focus, their shouts just dim noise. Isaac was concentrating, waiting for Burke to make a move.

He didn't have to wait long. They turned down a gravel driveway—two hundred meters to go, Isaac figured—and Burke kicked it into passing gear. Isaac stayed with him—for fifty meters or so. But then Burke pulled a step ahead, and two, and three. Isaac held it there, but he couldn't gain it back. He couldn't go any faster. He thought about next year. There would always be next year.

The faces on either side were closer now, pressing in, and Isaac heard his name. There was his dad, leaning out from the row of spectators on the left, hands cupped around his mouth. "Go, Isaac!" he shouted. "You can do it!"

The emptiness in Isaac's legs had spread to his gut. He ignored it, searched for a spark. He thought of the canyon, of Danny, of his dad. A hundred meters. That was all he needed to do.

He made up a step on Burke, and another, and another, and they were running shoulder to shoulder again. He waited for Burke to let him go, but Burke wouldn't. They had fifty meters left. Isaac could see the finish line. He blocked out everything else and concentrated on the tape stretched in front of him. He leaned, watched out of the corner of his eye as Burke drifted back. Isaac broke the tape and staggered to a stop.

Then his mom was there, and his dad, and Burke. "See you at state, Isaac," he said. Isaac watched him walk away, head up. He had a feeling that their next race wouldn't be any easier. But that didn't matter for now. He'd won the invitational.

Isaac's dad wrapped him up—sweat and all—in a

monster hug. "I'll be there, too, Isaac," he said. His voice sounded different—choked and shaky. Isaac blinked the salt away and studied his dad's face. Above the proud grin his dad's eyes were wet. "If—when—you get to the state meet, I'll figure out some way to get there."

Isaac felt light-headed, weak-kneed, but mostly warm inside—happier than he remembered ever being before. "That would be great," he said. His own throat felt lumpy, his voice thick. "I may need you at the finish again."

"You would have won it anyway."

Isaac thought his dad was right—that he would have found a way to win no matter who was standing on the sidelines. But having his dad there made the victory more special, made Isaac feel that the distance between them was just miles on the road, that they were still close after all.

● ● ●

He got to the track at the usual time Monday morning. He hadn't seen Danny after the race, so he was anxious to talk to him. But Danny wasn't there, and he didn't show up during the workout. Maybe he figured his job was over.

Isaac remembered the day he'd met Danny and

asked him where he lived. Danny had pointed in the direction of the tree line, the fields beyond. They'd never run that way. Maybe it was time to try. Maybe he could find Danny's house.

He left the track and jogged through the fields to a narrow, potholed road that led past a small cemetery and an abandoned farm. He reached the top of a hill and stopped. Nothing in the direction he was heading. He turned back, past the deserted farm, and cut through the cemetery entrance. He slowed, glancing at the headstones—weathered and faded and old.

But at the edge of the cemetery a newer stone caught his eye, and he stopped. It was small and simple, but the grass around it was newly trimmed, and a bouquet of fresh flowers lay against it. He read the name and the dates, and he stopped breathing. A chill shot up his spine.

"Danny LeGrand," the stone read. "Born November 2, 1954; Died November 1, 1975." Beneath the name and dates was an inscription: "He Runs in God's Country."

It couldn't be. But somehow Isaac knew it was true. He knew whose grave this was. He left the cemetery at a slow jog, not looking back. Then he picked up the pace, faster and faster, until he was sprinting across the field.

When he got back to the track, he cut straight across the infield toward home. At the bleachers he slowed, out of gas.

"Did you find him, Isaac?"

Isaac stopped. Coach Harrell stood up and walked toward him. In the dim light, through the fog that had descended on his senses, Isaac hadn't seen him sitting there.

Isaac hesitated, but he knew the answer. "Yeah," he said finally.

"It's been more than twenty years," the coach said. "But he was the best we ever had here—until now. Went to Oregon on scholarship. Only one besides you to ever go to the invitational. He must've been pretty impressed with you."

"You've seen him?"

"A few times. Thought I was losing my mind. When you told me what had happened—who was helping you—I felt better, in a way. But it was still hard to believe. Even now, I don't know if I can."

Isaac didn't know if he could, either. But what other choice did he have? He'd spent hours with Danny, listened to him, talked to him, run with him. "No other Danny around here?"

He saw the coach smile. "What do you think?"

Isaac shrugged. He didn't know why he'd bothered

to ask. "How did he die?"

"The canyon. The south wall. Home for the week-end on a day like today. He loved it there. He loved the challenge. But the ice got him. And a hundred-foot fall."

The south wall. Isaac pictured it; he imagined Danny racing down its narrow trail on a grey winter morning, slipping and tumbling down its steep, icy face. The thought tore at Isaac's insides. Did he die right away, or did he lie there, waiting for someone who never arrived? "Do you think he'll come back?"

"Don't know. Maybe he was just waiting around to help somebody—to help you." He stuck out his hand, and Isaac took it. "Great job this weekend, Isaac," he said. "Nobody else here has ever done it."

"Not Danny?"

"He took second. The hill got him. He couldn't quite come back."

Isaac thought of the hill, the pain. He thought of the canyon. "I gotta go," he said, and started across the field.

"Take it easy, Isaac," the coach said.

Isaac barely heard him. He was moving now, length-ening his stride, heading for the canyon. He'd go alone, but maybe he'd meet up with somebody on the way. Maybe he would.